Always Read The Small Talk

Beatrice Felicity Cadwallader-Smythe

To Everyone Trapped in Coffee Mornings Everywhere.

'All that is solid melts into air...' Karl Marx 1848

CONTENTS

Chapter One

One never expects a cry for help on a Wednesday. Wednesdays are, after all, a day for reflecting on how, if at all, the week has so far progressed our lives' dreams and for pondering on how it is that the last few days have snuck across one's life leaving hardly a trace; a time for gathering one's strength for the final stretch to the weekend when, hopefully, some nice things will happen – or at least some things one might remember when Wednesday comes around once again, as it invariably does, to challenge us as to the purpose of one's life and we need something, at least, by way of an answer.

But a cry for help it most certainly was.

It was Angela. I need to tell you about Angela – or Angie as she sometimes likes to be called when she is feeling risqué – and myself: We are old friends. Best friends. Or, at least, we have known each other a long time. Or, at least, we have associated with each other in various circumstances down the years and remained on amicable terms. Or, at least, we have discussed most subjects it is deemed necessary to have discussed whilst still keeping within the confines of polite society, which is to say, hardly anything of importance or interest but everything of fashion and inconsequence: so we knew each other, to summarise, as well as it is possible to know each other without breaking the boundaries of good manners, common decency, polite small talk and the rituals of coffee morning or dinner party – which is to say, hardly at all.

So the phone call was something of a surprise.

"Beth! Hello! It's Angela. Would you like to come round for a coffee?"

Her voice, I felt, was a tad higher in tone than was absolutely necessary in the apparent circumstances and from where I was sitting I could see that the monthly coffee-morning was circled on the kitchen calendar for the following week nor was it either of our turns to do the supper-party plus the charity – volunteers' ladies' group wasn't due for another fortnight – so I knew immediately that something was wrong. I had heard rumours, of course, as one always does – one of the other ladies had rung me to let me know what she had heard only two days previously – but I hadn't paid too much attention as this particular lady was always hearing things which turned out not to be 'things' at all (I think she just makes excuses to phone people actually) but it occurred to me now that maybe, this time, the rumours were true and something might, against all expectations, considerations of decorum or respect for our social schedule, have actually happened.

"Angela? You alright, my dear?" I said.

I felt a lapse into the vernacular, affectionate and informal was perhaps permissible in the circumstances.

"Yes – I'm fine, absolutely fine – sorry to bother you – just wanting a chat really – hope you don't mind – would you like to come round?"

So the rumours were true.

"I'll be round in ten minutes." This could be good, I thought.

I dropped the magazine I'd been scanning, downed the usual small, afternoon-sherry in one, switched off the radio play I'd been half listening to, reversed the car out of the garage and left.

We are best friends after all.

When I arrived at Angie's it all looked normal: the houses in the smart cul-de-sac all looked as smart cul-de-sac houses ought to look and Angela's was no exception. I knew which one was hers, as I always did, by its number next to the garage wall. All looked as it should – as it invariably did.

But as I walked up to the front door and pressed on the bell, suddenly I saw, through the frosted glass panel, with its pattern of fluttering doves and intertwined daisies (Angela having gone through a flower-arranging phase and her husband one of ornithology) a strange, dark shape lying at the bottom of the stairs.

That was unusual.

I rang the bell again, more insistently and called out, "Angela! It's me – Beth!" – wondering whether to smash the glass and with what. One of the gnomes on the lawn looked useful but before I could make a decision the door opened and Angela was there – quite upright and alive.

"Hello, Beth! How nice to see you! Do come in!" She seemed in a hurry to get back to whatever she'd been doing on my arrival as she started back down the hallway straightaway.

Following after her, I glanced down at the bottom of the stairs and saw an amorphous heap of apparently random, household objects piled at the foot of the stairs on top of a suitcase – making the dark blurred shape which I had seen through the glass.

She had gone into the living room.

"Hello," I said, "for a moment I wondered…" but she had settled into a chair calling. "Come in, I'm just watching this," over her shoulder.

So I did.

The television was on and the screen was flickering black and white.

"Thanks so much for coming," she said, over her shoulder, breezily," I just don't want to miss this," she continued, eyes fixing on the screen as she settled into the armchair.

The sense of emergency having somewhat evaporated I sat down on the sofa to see what was so fascinating.

On the screen were two people: a man with a mac, a trilby and an intense expression and a woman in a hat, a smart suit and an expression of slight bewilderment, in a familiar scene. While I watched, an aeroplane took off into a foggy night while the mac-and-be-trilby-ed character walked away into the fog with a man in a uniform and the credits came up.

"Oh I do love that, don't you?" Angela breathed, "My absolute *favourite*!"

She was still gazing at the screen as the credits rolled.

"Er yes, never gets old, does it," I managed, having seen *'Casablanca'* a few times down the decades. "I never *can* guess what will happen next. You, er, mentioned coffee?" I hinted.

She was still rapturising – if there is such a word.

"Oh it's the most fabulous love story *ever*!" she sighed.

I was sceptical, "Really? I thought it was about a whole lot of refugees all trying to escape from… something or other?"

"Oh *yes* – they *are* refugees, "she conceded" – but *nice* ones – with nice clothes and everything – the Nazis have just invaded everywhere and are killing everybody so everyone is trying to get away or fight them and stop them – but that's not the *important* story – the *main* thing is about Ilsa and Rick, you see?"

"Right! It *is* the 'hill of beans' that matters after all – I'll drink to that… could I?"

She took the hint and brought the necessary – the real stuff I was relieved to see – sometimes one gets fobbed off in less formal gatherings with powders or granules and such nonsense and I hate it when standards are allowed to slide.

"Biccie?" she offered.

I declined and noticed that they were not on the usual doilied plate. The cups, though, were at least matching so it looked as though the crisis had been diverted and she hadn't completely lost all sense of propriety.

There was a short silence.

"Well," she said at last, having clicked off the screen which was offering, or threatening, to replay the Great Classic or provide Selected Scenes, "I'm wondering if you can help me?"

"Anything my dear – just name it," I said, hoping I didn't sound too sincere or that I'd have to retract too quickly.

"I'm a bit like 'Ilsa' in 'Casablanca', you see – I have to make a choice," she said and took a sip of coffee.

"Oh?" This sounded promising. We hadn't had a decent sex-scandal in the offing since Georgina had made off with her window cleaner and that had only been for a fortnight but we still talked about it. (Apparently he hadn't been a Shakespearian actor doing research for a new role as window cleaner after all so she had returned, disappointed in some ways but not, I had suspected at the time, in others.)

"You see," Angie continued on the scandal in hand, "she loves *him* and he loves *her* – but they can't be together because…"

"Yeh –I know –," I interrupted, "'three people's little lives' – 'hill of beans' – 'crazy world' – blah-de-blah… They haven't updated it yet then?"

"Well, it's a bit more moving than that," Angie sounded offended, "I know *exactly* how she feels, "she said dramatically, "Torn between two lovers!"

"You do?" I said, "Better weekend than usual then?" I prompted, hopefully. I knew nothing of her private life beyond the usual window dressing of 'happy marriage with kids' 'so this promised to be more interesting than almost any of our previous conversations – excepting, perhaps, for the one when we had all speculated about a friend, Edwina's, singles' holiday – but that had been years ago and it had turned out that she had thoroughly enjoyed the archaeological dig for itself without any need for embellishments after all, despite all our fevered speculations.

Angela was refilling her cup and did not elaborate so I prompted,

"So… like Ilsa… you don't know whether to love the heroic freedom fighter, What-is-name or the sexy lounge lizard, Rick? Which one is Martin supposed to be?"

I was finding it difficult to imagine Martin, her bland husband, taking on the Nazis, risking life and limb and fighting for freedom – if the battle interfered for more than five minutes with his model-making, crosswords or number puzzles – but I couldn't see him running a café-bar either.

"Yes," said Angela, mournfully, "Ilsa doesn't know which *man* to be with – and I can't choose which *flat* to move into. It's the same you see."

Because this was a bit of a comedown in the gossip department, I tried not to show my disappointment as I pushed away various fond imaginings of other, more complex choices we are sometimes all called upon to make – if we're lucky.

"I don't think Ilsa had to choose a flat," I suggested.

"Well, she might have done," Angela was defensive, "if her and Rick had settled down together – they'd have had to live *somewhere*! I was just saying – Ingrid Bergman and me – she doesn't know which man she wants to run into the sunset with – and I don't know which flat downtown I want to move into. It's the same you see."

"Yes," I said (well, I had to agree), "That could even be the sequel... *'Casablanca 2':* Rick and Ingrid set up house together – they could maybe open a teashop?"

Angela frowned. "No, I don't think that would work," she said doubtfully. "Unless," she brightened, "they made it a musical?"

But she looked doubtful at the idea. "Not much adventure in that though," she muttered.

"Life isn't about adventure, dear," I said, reassuringly.

I didn't want to explore the musical option further anyway, so yanked the conversation into the present and firmly away from the image of Humphrey Bogart, in his Macintosh and trilby, tap-dancing.

"But you live *here*," I hauled us back to the present scenario, gesturing at the comfort around us. "So –

why are you choosing a flat."

She looked at me and paused as if weighing me up. Our long relationship seemed to flicker in the air between us.

Then she said, "Because Martin... has gone. Elsewhere. Temporarily of course!" she added quickly.

So the rumour was true!

I hurried to present myself as naïve, uninformed and well-intentioned. It's a knack I have perfected.

"He's on holiday?" I ventured innocently.

Obviously I wouldn't tell her that I already knew – one must always protect one's sources.

"No... he's – My husband has... Martin has met... someone. ... Someone *else*."

This was news. I'd often wondered how people like Martin ever met *someone* never mind someone *else*. Bland is the word you would need to describe Martin, should you ever need to do so – although that circumstance would also seem improbable as he was rarely a topic of any conversation of which I'd been a party. You also wouldn't need 'interesting' or 'attractive'. They would be redundant words. As would 'unpredictable'.

I made some sympathetic noises and some others of disbelief and outrage for which the occasion did seem to call. She dabbed at her eyes. I had seen this scenario many times – albeit with different personnel.

But then I spotted the flaw in her plan for moving house so expeditiously. I had come across the same mistake so often, professionally.

"Yes," I said, "but *he'll* have to support *you* because *he's* the one who's left…"

Having a solicitor as a husband does have its advantages. I knew about such things. Being an estate – agent, like I am, often brings you into close range of the harsh realities of other people's lives – I had long enjoyed this aspect of my job – but having a solicitor as a husband brings one even closer – and you are able to pay all the bills from the fruits of some of the harvest and have quite a bit left over for taking out quite a lot of the harsh realities from one's own existence.

"He hasn't *left!*" Angela said – a bit sharpish I felt.

"Oh," I backtracked, "I thought… you said… thought he had gone?"

I gestured weakly, indicating the general lack of Martins in the room.

"This is *temporary!*" she said, emphatically, putting her cup of coffee down quite firmly and spilling a little into the saucer. I had never seen her like this.

"He's having a *'fling',* I believe it's called," she continued. "That is ALL! So I just need somewhere else to live for a while so he knows I'm not just waiting here for him – like a pathetic little housewife – that'll rattle him – and then he'll be *back* – you'll see!"

"Oh," I said, as if I did see (although I didn't) and nodded.

"So I don't want to ask him for money or alley-money or whatever it is or go to court because that would make it all seem more than it is – it would all be final and legal and permanent – and it ISN'T! This is just a temporary glitch in our relationship which is otherwise *perfect*!"

I had come across denial before and, personally, have plenty of time for it as it seemed to me to provide a necessary cushion between us and the nastier aspects of life until we're in a fit state to deal with them – if we ever are. A life replete with denial has always seemed to me to be rather appealing given the state of much of reality.

A thought occurred.

"Is that why there's a heap of things at the bottom of the stairs? And a suitcase?" I enquired.

"Yes! That's right!" Angie agreed, "I'm moving on! That's my whole new life! The new *me*!"

She had stood up dramatically at this point and flung her hair back as if to fling it off her face. (It hadn't been on her face but one often has to improvise when the moment demands.)

"That small heap of stuff at the bottom of the stairs?" I continued, "With the toaster and the lamp?"

"Yes."

"And the slippers?"

"Yes!"

"Not much in it then – this new life? It's a very small pile."

"I won't be *needing* much! I want life – not *things*! I want the *world*!"

Angela walked over to the patio window at the opposite end of the living room from the telly and threw her arms wide towards the view outside. A dog had just been about to squat on the lawn outside but, alarmed at her sudden appearance, jumped away and slunk towards the gate wearing a guilty expression. Some small drops of coffee had flown out of her cup during the arm-throwing gesture and had spattered the curtain on that side but I didn't feel it was the time to mention it. The lawn and the hedges outside the window looked kempt and domesticated – unsuspecting of the high drama which was being directed towards them as symbols of the wide, wild world of untold adventures at that moment.

"I," she declared, "am heading to pastures new – I won't be needing much – I am leaving this materialistic world – I won't be tied down with worldly possessions and the baggage of the past!"

It was quite impressive as a grand statement. It might have been even more impressive if she had, at that moment, swung astride a magnificent, skittish stallion – which reared on its hind legs, nearly throwing her – and urged it into a headlong gallop towards a far horizon. But she didn't. She straightened one of the curtains instead.

"So… you're selling this place?" I ventured. "Casting off worldly goods?"

I was quite impressed.

"Selling? Hell, no!" she said, "I can get a *lot* more for it renting it out! Rents are sky-high at the moment – house-prices low – I could clean up!"

"Right!" I said, feeling myself to be in familiar territory. Our office does rentals as well so at least there was a chance of a commission and my day would not be entirely wasted.

"I'm heading off into a whole new life! Temporarily," she declared looking at me defiantly as if I was about to cross her. I sipped my coffee in what I hoped was an appeasing and accepting, philosophical sort of way – which takes a bit of pulling off without spillage, I can tell you.

"This little pile of simple belongings is all I need for my new life of wild adventure and discovery," she ended, breathlessly, waving her arm in the direction of the small heap at the foot of the stairs

"I see. You're taking your gardening gloves then?" A dainty pair, green and flowery, was visible amidst the pile.

"Yes of course."

"Right – new adventures in the horticultural department anyway! Great! How can I help?"

I was dying to know more about the mysterious 'other woman' who had been lumbered with, sorry I mean 'ran off with', the spectacularly un-gorgeous Martin but didn't feel it polite to wade right in there with blunt questions so bided my time.

"Well," she said, "… you're my oldest friend," (I was flattered at this – if a little alarmed) "and – I wanted to… talk to someone about all this – someone I could trust and – the house – I want to rent it out but I want to make it *look* as if I'm selling it – you see? But not sell it. That's something you could help me with?"

"Oh?" This sounded intricate. (I'm not keen on 'intricate'. It often ends in 'messy' – and by a short-cut.)

"Not really *sell* it," she clarified, "I mean – the market's totally flat at the moment – I checked – so by the time anyone comes to even look at it Martin will be back with his tail between his legs begging for forgiveness".

"An appealing image," I had to admit.

"So if you could just make it look as if I *am* selling it – with a board and everything – and make sure he knows that I am – but I won't be."

'Well bang goes my commission', I thought – but didn't say out loud. I was her oldest friend after all.

"So, please," she went on," help me choose a flat – I move out – House goes on the market with your company – you make sure it doesn't sell"…

"Yes, I'm good at that." She missed the hint of sarcasm in my voice.

"… Martin hears about it – and my wild new life… He realises what he is missing – he comes back – all is back to how it should be – normal."

"And that's what you want?" I queried. The alternative was, after all, the single life – supported financially by Martin: Life and a Whole New Beginning. What was not to like, I pondered.

"Of course that's what I want! Martin back and all back to normal. Me and Martin in *our* house!" she declared.

"Martin and I," I corrected.

What was so great about 'normal' she didn't elaborate. She was obviously seeing things differently to how they looked from where I was standing. I always find it irritating when people do that

"Right – good!" I said.

Having Martin back was what she wanted, for whatever reason, and who was I to argue? Some people like sparkling sweet wine after all – not anybody I know, certainly, that I'm aware of, but I had seen it in shops so somebody had to be buying it. And Angela had bought Martin, obviously she still thought she had a bargain and not some tasteless plonk left at the bottom of the barrel which nobody else had wanted.

I was irked at my Wednesday having been disturbed without any emergency or even any hot gossip having been provided.

"So, that's the plan?" I summarised, "the choice – just flats – no new love affairs then? No new love in your life?"

"Well, no, of course not, Beth!" Angela sounded shocked. I had come across her rather straight-laced views before, "I'm a married woman! Martin's only been gone a few weeks!"

"Well – time to crack on," I answered. "At our time of life we can't afford to hang about."

She tossed her head as if to fling her hair back off her face again but this time in an angry sort of way which didn't work very well as she was still wearing her Alice band so her hair still wasn't anywhere near her face – but the gesture indicated offence having been taken, if I read it rightly. To underline this she said with emphasis, "I'm *not* that superficial – and this marriage is *not* over."

I grimaced. She had, after all, however unwittingly, touched a nerve.

"Well," I ventured, "some people don't wait for their marriages to be over…?"

She looked at me – her eyes not exactly blazing but looking a little warmer than usual.

"Yes I know," she said, "But I am not *that* kind of woman any more than you are, Beth, and I'm surprised at you suggesting such a thing!"

She went out to the hallway and started putting her new life into its suitcase.

I could have said more but felt she had already had enough surprises for one day.

I looked at the pile of belongings speculatively, "That's quite a small pile of things you're taking with you – if that's your new life?"

"Yes – I'm travelling light. Freedom at last! This is the new me! Not tied to great piles of material wealth! Off you lendings!"

"What if he *doesn't* come back? What about all your beautiful furniture? And the house? Aren't you going to fight Martin for them?" I asked.

"What? No way! I'm not getting into some sordid scrap over whose is what... that would only bring me down to his level!"

She was offended again.

"Well that's very high minded and spiritual of you – is he taking it all to *his* new place then?" I asked.

"No way – it's staying right here – he's not getting his hands on it – I can rent this place out for a *lot* more if it's furnished."

"Ah," I was reassured, "High-minded and spiritual – but also reassuringly mercenary – could be a new religion. But what if Martin comes to pick it up?"

"No problem – I've had the locks changed," she said, brusquely.

Again, I was impressed.

"You're leaving a lot behind," I speculated, eyeing the designer carpets, cushions and must-have prints – ghastly, of course, but all the rage.

She looked affronted, "I'm not taking it with me. The new flat is in the dock area anyway. You know the sort of people down there – they might nick it. They don't have nice things – wouldn't appreciate them if they did – Anyway this is history – my *past*. The old me – I'm going to change: I'm leaving it here to rot and decay like an old skin – for six months anyway – while the new me changes – blossoms and spreads its wings – like a new rose rising from the ashes like a butterfly changing its spots."

I was impressed again, "Quite a complicated change then. What about this?" I picked up an object from a shelf.

She winced, "Well no I'm not taking *that*! That ghastly thing! Horrible! Don't know why… Oh." She stopped, remembering.

"That was what I made in one of my first pottery classes wasn't it?" I ventured.

"Oh THAT!" she recovered quickly. "Oh I thought you meant *that*," she pointed vaguely. "Oh of course I'm taking THAT! Yes – be the centre piece in my new hallway!"

"Don't see why?" I said. "It's ghastly! Worst thing I ever made!"

She laughed at that. "How are your evening classes going?"

"Oh fine," I said, "keeps me out of mischief. Keeps me busy. You ready for off then?"

"I suppose so. I'm meeting the letting agency reps down there. Thanks for coming with me." She headed towards the door and opened it. Then she sighed, looked back at the living room and hesitated.

"Such enthusiasm!" I urged. "Your carriage awaits

— ready to start your whole new life! You're moving on! It's what you're supposed to do in a crisis!" I did have another commitment later on, after all and didn't have all day.

"Yes." She sighed again, "Fancy another coffee?"

"Shouldn't we get going? What time you meeting the agent?"

"Oh anytime," she had no sense of urgency, "they said just call in — the flats are just round the corner. Their young men show you round."

"How many are you looking at? Flats I mean — not young men! Although if we've got time…!"

But she didn't laugh —just looked at me, puzzled.

"Do you know where we're going?" I said, to change the subject.

"Sort of. I've got an A-Z. Here…"

"Oh good. An A-Z. Can't possibly get lost then! Many flats to see?" I was thinking of the time.

"Just two," Angela said, "I've narrowed it down — the ones I like are down here — near the old dockland — see?"

She had a page open in the A-Z — it was a page I had looked at before and I suppressed a shudder.

"I rented out a flat around there to a client a while ago," I said in a cautionary tone.

21

She probably felt obliged to ask, "And what was wrong with it?"

"Oh, nothing much – just the price, the damp, the traffic noise, the fumes, the mice inside, the rats outside and the creepy landlord," I summarised, briefly.

"Ah!" she said, carrying on packing the case – pushing in a flowery toiletry bag.

"That hasn't put you off?" I asked.

"No – that's the area I want!" She sounded quite decided.

"Hmm," I suspected a motive. "Very trendy."

"That's right! Trendy! That's what I want!"

"If a bit loud at night," I informed her."All those clubs and pubs."

"You know it?"

"I've passed through it," I said, vaguely.

"Exactly!" she said, as if she had proved a point.

"You giving up sleep as well?" I queried.

"Hopefully, yes. That'll show him!" She closed the suitcase and heaved it towards the door.

"Show who? I mean whom?" I asked, losing my sense of the grammatical among all the dramatic goings on.

"Well Martin of course!"

"Show him what?"

She looked at me as if exasperated, "That I'm young and free and single and having a wild time of course!"

I didn't say anything.

"Well, young-ish and wild-ish anyway," she conceded.

"So is Martin living down there now as well then? With his floozie? Has she got a flat down there?"

Was Angela planning to park on their doorstep, I wondered. That wouldn't end well, I thought.

She hesitated.

"There's something I need to tell you about the 'floozie'," she said.

'Finally!' I thought – but didn't say. I'm not good at patience and had to congratulate myself on my present forbearance.

"Fire away!" I said, generously, agog for salacious details.

"Actually, I don't think anyone says 'floozie' anymore," she began.

"I know," I agreed, "I said it ironically," I lied smoothly, "so... what's her name? Is she someone from work? I bet she is! It's always…"

"Allan," said Angela.

"Allan?"

"Yes, Allan."

"Who's Allan?"

"He's Allan. Allan. The floozie. He's Allan."

"No one says…"

"I know they don't! Can you be a floozie if you're a man?"

"I don't think so. A *man*?"

"Yes. His name's Allan."

I was beginning to spot a theme.

"Not 'she' then?"

"No. He."

"Allan's a he?"

"Well how many she's do you know called Allan?"

She had a point there. I couldn't think of one.

"So… she's not 'she' then?"

"No. He's a 'he.' Allan's a he. He… Allan. He. Is. Allan."

I could almost immediately sense that I'd hit on a sore spot.

"Right!" I said.

"And yes he did."

"Did what?"

"That's where he met him."

"Who met who?" I was still tripping over the pronouns.

"Whom," she corrected, "Martin met Allan. Or Allan met Martin. At work. They work where I work. He met him. Or he met him. Whichever way round you put it."

That was true. Pronouns are so limiting. They had met each other.

"Right!" I was determined not to be phased until she was.

"You've already said 'Right!'… Say something else," she demanded.

"So… moving on… why are you moving downtown? Are they living there? Is that Martin's new place? Or Allan's…?"

"No," she said, "his new place is in suburbia – Martin couldn't live anywhere else. Allan's flat."

"Is he?"

"No," she said, "he's *got* a flat. Very smart too. Good area."

"Him and Martin have got a flat already?" I was astounded.

This was a bit fast. This sounded more serious. This did not sound fling-y. (If there is such a word.)

"Yes," she conceded, "so… they share a flat together – doesn't signify."

"Together?" I needed clarification. It did seem to signify to me.

"Yes of course together. Together, but – temporarily of course – that's the point! And this is a small town – word soon gets around."

"About what?"

"About *me*," she said, "– about my whole new life – They'll soon hear."

I nodded. "Of course they will. Why wouldn't they? What do you mean?"

I had a sudden mental image of Martin and his Allan sitting at breakfast over toast and the morning papers in their new flat being roused from domestic revelry by a clarion call announcing some astonishing news through their letterbox; news of such magnitude that it shatters their whole world: Angela having moved to a flat.

She nodded. "That's the plan!"

"There's a plan?"

She looked impatiently at me as if I was being obtuse.

"Yes! Of course there's a plan! This is the plan: Martin'll realise what he's lost. He'll hear about my whole new life. I'll be having good times – running

26

wild! That'll show him! He'll realise his mistake and kaboom! – we'll be back together in no time."

"Kaboom?"

"Yes, kaboom!"

"I don't think anybody says…"

"I don't *care* what anybody says. He'll be devastated when he hears I've moved on and he'll be *desperate* to get me back." She was quite certain about this.

"That's the plan?"

I had spotted a teeny – tiny flaw in it but felt it would be unsporting to point it out at this moment.

"Yes – that's the plan!"

I spotted a light. "Hmm – Have these flats got two bedrooms?" I asked.

"No, can't afford that," she said and the light expired, "'studios' I think they call them. Bedsits with a toilet attached from what I've seen. Why?"

"Well," I had to be sure not to sound too keen at this point, "you know, just if you needed any company – if I'm going to support you… in your new life and adventures – I thought you might want a chaperone – and I'd maybe need to sometimes stop over… at least." I left the hint hanging in mid-air.

She looked at me, surprised. "Well that's very kind

of you – I hadn't thought to ask but now you mention it. But…"

I had anticipated a 'but' and was quick off the mark.

"Just to keep you safe" I went on,… "come out with you, sometimes won't I? Look after you. Be your companion in this whole new life?"

"Ooh thanks!" said Angela. "Thank you! You are such a brick!"

I winced. "Not sure anyone says that any more either."

"Angel then. You're an angel!"

That was worse than 'brick' but I let it pass.

"It'll be great!" she went on. "Come aboard!! Good ship Wild Times and Hooray for the single life! O it'll be fun. Angie and Beth – out on the town. You'll just need a futon or a blow-up mattress to crash out in the living room – I'll soon get that sorted. But… will Frank be alright with that? Won't feel abandoned? The 'deserted husband'?" she frowned.

"No, I shouldn't think so." It was my turn to be certain. "Don't think anyone says, 'crash out' anymore either," I pointed out.

I decided that I'd go with the flow and sort out details later. After all, at school a friend and I had perfected the art of telling the hockey teacher we were doing netball and the netball teacher we were doing hockey and then sloping off to the high street café for a quiet smoke – so I knew what could be done.

"You sure?" she queried.

"Well, nobody I know does anyway… I think they say 'stay at my place' rather than 'crash'." I was confident in this.

"No," she said, "I meant about Frank minding you coming out with me and staying over?"

I waved a dismissive hand with authority. "Oh no, not at all, he's not that observant anyway – and he's got a golfing tournament all Summer – won't even notice I'm gone – Doesn't usually anyway," I muttered," Did your new tenants come round? What are they like?"

"Not yet - coming at the weekend," she propped the suitcase by the door and got her jacket on.

"Of course – no worries – It'll be snapped up I expect – by anyone wanting the quiet life-temporarily."

"Yes – quiet, respectable – boring. They're welcome to it Beth! I'm outa here!"

She was being dramatic again, punching the air – with her arm still halfway in the sleeve and snagging the seam.

"Yes –" I encouraged. "As you disappear over the horizon into your whole new beginnings."

She caught the spirit, "Yes! Out of the cul-de-sac

into the fast lane!" She grabbed up the suitcase and swung it over her shoulder.

"Bye-bye boring old house!" I joined in.

"Well, just au revoir," she said, lowering her fist a little. "I'm only doing this to get Martin back of course."

"Yes of course," for a moment I had actually forgotten. "Only temporarily into a wild new future – back quite soon. Quite a short, whole, new, wild future."

"Yes – a few weeks should do it. Maybe a month. Martin and Allan have just gone on holiday – by the time they're back I'd like to be living the bright life and have them all talking about me at work – you see – for a month – this fling of theirs will be over by then."

"So… A whole new wild future – for four weeks," I enthused. "Temporarily wild! Great! And I'm only coming along to help you. In your new single life. To get you back with Martin. Of course. But… you're looking at new flats today and you haven't got a tenant yet?"

Angie shrugged, "I don't want to rush these things."

"Angie, if you're moving into the fast lane, 'rushing things' kind of goes with the territory – last I heard," I hinted, helpfully.

She didn't look happy and put the suitcase down again.

"Well it all seems a bit extreme – having strangers living in our house."

"Having bailiffs moving about in it is a bit of a downer too." I put on my professional salesperson voice, "Someone has to pay the mortgage – you'll be paying rent – you've got to do *something* – renting this place out – good plan – just while Martin's away. Because you want to get him back – and this is all part of the plan."

"It just seems so sad." She leaned against the doorpost.

I said, quite harshly, "Yeah – try getting repossessed – that's sad too."

"Strangers in our house," she went on, "using our things!"

"Or bailiffs in your house," I rejoined, "… *taking* your things. A choice we all have to make."

But she was reminiscing and had gone all dreamy eyed.

She carried her case back along the hallway and back into the lounge and sat down, looking around her although it was all the same as previously.

I sat down too.

"I need a minute," she said.

She sighed. "It only seems five minutes since we moved in here – not 20 years – we were so *passionate* – making love all over the furniture – no don't worry – not there – and walking around naked in our own little house."

I wanted to say that five bedrooms, three bathrooms and two receptions didn't count as all that little but I didn't want to spoil the moment.

"How the years must have flown by!" I said.

She frowned, "Oh no – that was just the first week, then we had to get back to the office. It *was* a lovely week though."

"Lovely," I echoed, trying hard to get certain images out of my mind and looking pointedly away from the dining table. "What are these flats you're looking at then?"

Angela fetched a sheaf of newspaper out of her shoulder bag.

"Here's the ads – I've circled them."

I took the papers. This was of professional interest too – seeing what other agencies were getting away with fobbing – off as habitable these days and at what price.

"Let's see – 'Nice flat-let, central location' and… 'Nice flat-let, central location – not much to choose between them really – if you're looking for a nice flat-let – in a central location. Flat-*let*?"

She explained, "A bedsit with a window box attached plus a cupboard with a toilet in it. All I can afford. But this is not just a flat!"

"No," I agreed. I did know the term and what it signified. "It's a flat-*let*!"

"No it's a *statement*!" she declared.

"A state-let?" I suggested.

"A statement! A doorway – into my new life! A new un-trodden path – into the unexplored –un-tamed, un-chartered. My new future! At least for six – months. Minimum tenancy – it says there," she pointed.

"And then what? Six months go by quite fast in my experience."

"Well, back here of *course*!" She was being patient again, "This fling of Martin's won't last long – you'll see. We'll be back here. But until then – a wild, unpredictable future beckons."

"For six months?"

She glanced at me. "Yes, I don't like un-predictable, you never know what's going to happen, so six months will be quite long enough."

That gave me a thought. "The future always *is* unpredictable isn't it? It's only looking back that you see what was coming. Just as well I suppose."

But Angela disagreed. "Mine hasn't been unpredictable. Totally *pre*-dictable. Twenty years of the same- old, same old… may as well have just shovelled the day before into the next one – you couldn't tell the difference between them – boring, boring, boring. Get up, go to work, get up, go to work… Make dinner. Oh, Beth, *why* did he leave me?" She put her hands up to her forehead.

I floundered around to avoid the obvious.

"Er well," I was inspired. "Life is so full of mysteries isn't it? Whoever could have seen that coming? You had so much in common you and Martin after all."

Angela nodded enthusiastically. "We did! We had everything – a job each, a house, money, a child. We were fit and healthy. We did sex. We had friends. Not very good ones but they were there."

"Thanks," I said, coldly.

"Not you," she flustered, "– the others."

"I didn't know there were any others," but she pretended not to hear.

"Well, we were busy," she went on, "and there was always something good on the telly. We had everything, me and Martin."

"Martin and I," I corrected.

"Yes," she frowned, "you and Frank you mean.

Even having a child was fun… sometimes."

She sighed again. I glanced at the clock.

"Our son, Hugo!" she went on, not taking the hint, "now he's all grown up and living on another continent and we hardly ever see him – but it was nice while it lasted. Taking him to school – picking him up from school – arguing over which programmes he could watch, what vegetables he had to eat," she paused and hit a tragic note,"– all *gone* now! Oh Beth – Why did my Martin leave me?"

I picked up my bag by way of a prompt, "Oh, I don't know Angela – some people just want more."

"More what?" she demanded. "What else *is* there?"

That was my cue. "Well, that's what we're… what *you're* going to find out. And I'm going to help you. All set to go then?" I prompted again.

She picked up her bag again and stood up. I stood up too.

"Thanks for coming with me, Beth. But let's go by bus. I should get used to going by bus – now I'm selling the car."

I sat back down again.

I was shocked. I believe I might have gaped at this point.

"You're selling the *car*?"

"Yes," she was all wide eyed and quite innocent of the travesty she had uttered.

"I've got to economise," she wittered on. "Buses are about every twenty minutes aren't they? I'll just see if I've got change. Conductors never have enough change do they?"

"Conductors? Every twenty minutes? When was the last time *you* were on a bus? They don't have conductors anymore; and never mind '*change*' you'll need your American Express and round here they won't be every twenty minutes – more like about one every three days."

"Oh!" She looked shocked at the sudden cruelty of the world.

"No conductors?" she whispered.

"No," I confirmed, "they decided, in the customers' best interests and comfort, to get rid of them – it all adds to the sense of danger and excitement. We'll take my car."

She protested, "I need to get used to using public transport."

"But why?" I said, "I *do* hope we're still going to be friends!"

Nobody I knew travelled by bus except when they were plastered and then only ironically. The one thing I liked about buses is you could get on one and be safe in the knowledge that no one on there was anyone you knew. I didn't want that ruined by some eccentric pseudo-plan, however 'temporary.'

"And," I added, warming to my theme, "you'll find it costs ten times what it used to and there are only half as many running so they only ever go anywhere by the longest possible route."

"But there are always plenty of empty seats – I've noticed as they go past," she argued.

I agreed, "Yes – there *are* reasons for that. Like I said: costs ten times what it did, only half as many and always the longest route!"

She looked at me, "You seem to know a lot about it?"

I realised I had said too much.

"Yes well… I sometimes use buses for my evening classes – that way I can drink – or get a lift – or stay over or… whatever."

"Yes you've mentioned your evening classes sometimes at coffee mornings. They do sound interesting. Stay over? Where?"

"Oh here and there," I said vaguely. "Friendly lot evening class bunch… very friendly some of them… *So… have* you been on a bus lately?"

"Not lately," Angela admitted. "It's on my to-do list. One of the life-changing experiences that await me.

My bucket-list of new adventures and challenges!"

"Using a bus? Not canoeing up the Amazon then?"

She shook her head as if I'd suggested eating a mouse, "No!"

"Or hiking in the Himalayas?" I suggested.

"God, no! Why would I want to do *that*?"

This time it had been a lightly cooked gerbil.

I shrugged, "I don't know but people *do*. Either that or rampaging through what's left of the rainforests in hordes – all to get away from… whatever it is they want to get away from."

Angela looked curious, "What is it they want to get away from?"

I grimaced (elegantly, of course), "I don't know," I surmised. "Each other probably."

She looked out of the window. "I see, off they *go*! Off to the wild places! To the far away, hidden-away wonders of the world!"

I inclined my head, "Well, not so much – they're all packed solid nowadays with lost middle-aged folk trying to find themselves – and infecting all the locals while they look."

Angela bridled, "Middle-*youthed* – thank-you not middle aged! I'm *not* middle aged!"

"Of course you're not," I soothed, mentally doing

the maths of doubling what I guessed was her age and wondering if anyone *had* ever reached that number without actually having been freeze-dried. "Sorry – but isn't that part of your plan? Explore the world? More of a challenge than getting on a bus. I'd come with you – keep you company?"

That could be an adventure.

"Thanks but no," said Angela, "not really – I always get travel sick. I'll put kettle on. Top up?"

"Thanks. We're not in any rush then?" The clock was moving, after all, albeit extremely slowly, even for a Wednesday. Time always moved slowly in this house. I had noticed that previously.

"No!" she called back from the kitchen, "this is going to be the new me, Beth – no deadlines – no plans – no schedules – no rush."

Angela was being dramatic again.

"Bus timetables might be a bit of a problem then," I said pointedly.

"Oh – we can catch the next one," Angela brandished the coffee spoon, "I'm going to let the *real* me out at last!" she gushed.

"There's another one?" I feigned interest.

"Yes!" the coffee spoon was plunged into the sugar bowl, I wondered if she was being symbolic. "I'm going to trip the light fantastic. He won't know what hit him."

She was, I was glad to see, opening the biscuits at this point. (And about time!)

I rushed to catch up, "Who won't know what? What hit who?"

Or should that have been whom?

"Martin of course."

"You're going to *hit* him?"

"I'd like to." She struck a pose and the biscuits went everywhere, "Use my new found karate skills and throw him across a room and tread on him."

"You've been to karate classes?" I asked, impressed. I mean – you think you know someone, I thought silently, and it turns out…

She said, "No, but I've been watching lots of Jackie Chan films and it can't be all that difficult can it?" She was picking up the biscuits.

I recollected I had only ever been in the dining room or lounge before and had never witnessed goings – on in the kitchen before. Certain past mysteries about upset stomachs were happily being solved as we went along.

… and it turns out there is nothing about them which surprises you at all, I said in a psychic silent message to my coffee.

But she had raised a moot point. Working alongside exes is not recommended as a usual rule. Especially if they are one's underlings I have discovered -although that wasn't the case here.

"Is Martin still going to be working at your place?" I ventured. "It would help you move on if he got a different job. Or if you did. Seeing him every day might be difficult… seeing them together… If him and Allan are back from their holiday I mean… Just while this lasts," I added, keeping to her narrative that this was temporary.

"Yes, he'll still be there. Toad." She nibbled on a biscuit, "Yes. Maybe throwing him and Alan across the room is not such a good idea – I might be had up by Health and Safety – I might just quietly spill something on them at the water cooler instead. Something brightly coloured which won't come out."

"Good plan – Jackie Chan always improvises – not sure he's ever done that though. You could waylay them at the water-cooler with a cup of blackcurrant juice – it'd be a welcome home gift when the new loves get back from their honeymoon…"

I'd said the wrong thing again. She glowered, "Their cheap, sordid getaway if you don't mind, not *honeymoon*. And it's not *love* – how can it be? I'll be ready when they get back – give me something to look forward to. But at least the office gossip has moved on now. Me and Martin took everybody by surprise."

"Martin and *I*," I corrected, again.

She ignored me. She had no feeling for grammar.

"It was all anyone could talk about for two whole *days*. Ooh, Martin and Allan! Martin and Angela – ooh! – have you *heard*? Every time I walked into a room they all looked at me in total silence."

She looked whimsical and pained in a dramatic sort of way. "It was like being a celebrity. I could tell what they were thinking: 'That poor heroic woman – she's taking it so well – how does she maintain such *dignity*? How *could* he leave her? What a low-down *toad*! She's looking so regal in her suffering. Why would he leave such a wonderful woman!'"

"It was quite a chatty total silence then?" I noted.

"Well they were thinking something *like* that I'm sure," she said. "I could tell in their faces. And as soon as I left a room I knew they'd be at it – gossip – gossip – gossip – people love to pull down anyone in high office – it was mortifying – so unkind – so common and heartless… But now Stanley and Marjorie in accounts have copped off with each other so now everyone's got a new interest. Beryl's opened a sweepstake. I put a fiver on it lasting two weeks. He's married you know and *she's* no better than she ought to be – people say…"

"*So*," I interrupted, "Martin met this Allan at work?"

"Yes," she scowled, elegantly of course, and dumped milk into the coffee straight from the bottle out of the fridge. I reflected on how amazingly quickly some people's standards were dropped. "They met at work."

I spotted a way forward.

"But Martin's the company Psychologist isn't he? Couldn't you get him struck off for 'seeing' one of his clients – to use a euphemism."

Angela didn't look impressed. "Well I wouldn't do *that* – we'd be skint then wouldn't we? When he gets back I mean... I've got to plan ahead. Anyway, Allan *wasn't* one of his clients – they met at a works social, he said, when he finally confessed all – I'd known for ages he was carrying on with *somebody*. But I thought it was Marjorie in marketing. She carries on with *everybody*. I spent ages tracking her moves. Marketing indeed! I followed her around in my car whenever Martin went out."

"You could have been done for stalking!"

"Yes, but she just went shopping and flyposting for XR... I thought he'd fallen for her – everyone fancies her – 'Marjorie – in-Marketing' – all bob, boobs and eyeliner. It never occurred to me it was Allan in Accounts – all paunch, brogues and bald patch!"

"I reassured her, "Well why *would* it occur to you? Not anyone's obvious choice by the sound of him, I'd have thought. Love *is* blind after all…"

She put the biscuits away – rather energetically I thought and I still hadn't had one. "It *isn't* love! This is just a *fling* – an experiment – a mid-life thingy for Martin. Men always run off with younger women at his age."

"But Allan's a fellah. And he sounds a bit older – is he? That *is* a bit unusual – to run off with an older fellah. Especially when you *are* a fellah."

"Proves my point!" she responded, unfazed.

"Does it?" I didn't quite see how.

"But I'll show them!" She ignored me again.

"Of course you will."

She put the biscuit tin on the table absent-mindedly and I helped myself.

"Just because they're off 'skiing'," Angie went on. "And 'seeing the world'. And 'talking'. Do you know Martin actually said he talked more to Allan than he ever had to me?"

"When did he tell you that – and how long has this been going on – as the song says – him and this Allan?" I asked.

But she was in full seethe. "I've wasted years of my life with that man. I'll show him. I'll show him

44

'Talking'. I'll show him, 'Skiing'. I'm going to get him back you know."

"I thought you said it was boring being married to him?" I was trying to keep up at the same time as trying to find a biscuit that wasn't soggy.

"It was!" she snapped. "That's not the point! I *liked* being bored! It was *my* bored!"

I had to point out, "I thought you said it was a waste of your life?"

"I *liked* wasting it," she sipped her coffee, angrily, (I'd never thought sipping was something that could be done angrily but we live and learn.) "What else am I supposed to do with it?"

"Have you thought of evening classes?" I suggested.

She looked curious, "Evening classes?"

"Yes," I said cheerfully, "works for me. More interesting than you might think. You should try it."

"You've mentioned evening classes you go to before – Greek History isn't it?" she was mildly interested. This was one of the subjects safe enough for any dinner party.

"On a Tuesday yes. French for beginners on Wednesday, Medium-level Pottery on Thursday, Belly dancing Monday and Advanced Pottery on Friday – and in the last few years I did Beginners' Pottery, Watercolours and Spanish. Helps you it does –

learning stuff."

She looked at me in puzzlement. "How much do you want to know? I don't think I'd want to know all that! And you must be out nearly every night?"

I agreed. "Nearly – and there are other side benefits – meet new people, go new places, I like having a varied life."

She looked at me, "But doesn't Frank mind?"

I shrugged elegantly which was something I like to keep in practice, "Who can tell? I like evening classes – he likes golf and the golf club set."

"Right," she sounded doubtful. "But you're out every night?"

"It works for us. Keeps us together. We all have to do what's right for us."

Angie frowned, "Well I like being *married*," she said decidedly. "Ring on my finger; Coming home after work; Husband coming home after work; Steak and chips on a Friday; Salad on Tuesday. Sex on a Saturday. Sometimes. We used to go on holiday to Scotland." A thought occurred to her, "Oh, Beth! We'll never do that again... I'll never see the lonely, windswept lochs and wild, untamed mountains again!"

"Why – have the coach trips stopped running?" I asked.

She snorted, slightly, "I'm not going on coach trips

any more. I'm going to *hitchhike*!"

I spotted a flaw. "Angie you always take about four suitcases with you on holiday. You can't take four suitcases with you when you hitchhike. People object. You could only get lifts in artic lorries if you did."

"Then artic lorries it is! Or I'll get a rucksack! And I'm going to go on singles holidays, then-safaris into the wilderness – off the beaten track! Excitement and adventure!"

"Not that much excitement, though," I pointed out, "The unbeaten track is pretty much beaten to death now – in fact, it's mostly tarmacked and has service stations at regular intervals selling burgers. You can get package deals now to the Serengeti or Kathmandu. All found, English breakfasts and pub quizzes laid on."

"They sound nice," she perked up.

"Yes," I agreed, "except there's not much point going. Even to the Arctic – or Sahara. Or even Alaska."

She shuddered, "I wouldn't go anywhere like that anyway. You never know what might happen."

"Angela," I had to point out, "isn't that what adventure and excitement means? Not knowing what might happen?"

"Well I don't want *that* much excitement," she said decisively.

"Well how much then?" (I like things to be precise.)

"Well you know," she considered, vaguely," just a bit."

"Just a bit of excitement?"

"Yes, that's right," she agreed, "a bit. Just a bit – Enough to show Martin!"

"Show him what?" I asked, "that you're a *bit* exciting? Not sure that will grab his attention you know. Anyway – you should do this for yourself – for your own life. We do only get one… as far as we know."

"I *will* grab his attention." Angie declared, "I'll search out new experiences, new ways of looking at… life and things – I'll *show* him. Exploring the unknown, finding new meaning to life. Find out more about myself – the *real* me! Search out the… hidden depths and meanings." She took another biscuit.

I considered. "You sure that's such a good idea? Anyway, good relationships are supposed to help you do that – search out new aspects of life – find things out about yourself." I'd read that somewhere but had never believed it.

"Me and Martin did searching!" she declared, "*Plenty* of searching!"

"Martin and I," I corrected, again, "and searching for the remote down the back of the couch doesn't count."

Immediately she was on the defensive. "We used to

watch nature programmes – they took us all over the world – snow leopards in the Himalayas; Tigers in India – whales in the sea… Steve Batchell… in his shorts…"

I nodded, "I wondered why you loved those programmes so much."

"Yes," she looked rueful, "and I'm getting an idea why Martin was so keen too. But I wanted to do *more* – I wanted to *go* on Safaris – Martin never did – he said it's never like that in real life… travel… just loads of waiting around in airports then glimpses of frightened animals in the distance from the back of your minibus – in traffic jams across the savannah."

"Well there you are then!" I saw light at the end of the tunnel, "he's held you back all these years – now's your big chance! He's off with this Allan – to all new adventures – time for you to have adventures in the world. Just temporarily – while they're having a fling – in their flat. "I ended lamely, seeing the look on her face. "Is it Allan's flat – it might be too small for two of them?"

"No, they chose it for the two of them. Allan's wife's moving out too. They're selling the house."

"Allan was married too? I mean – *is* married – *is*, of course! My! Quite a lot of people being surprised." I floundered. I saw another light, "Well that's handy. She could move in here and rent your place!"

Wrong again.

"No she *couldn't*!" Angie said angrily, "I'm not renting this place out to some middle-aged failure who couldn't even keep hold of her man. And let him get off with *mine*. It's her *fault*! If she'd been a good wife to her Allan he wouldn't have wanted to go off with my Martin!"

I hesitated, "I'm not *sure* that's how it works but yes, that's one theory."

"Well why else has this happened?" she demanded.

"Well, Angela, People do *change* – people move on – relationships end – people fall in love –and fall *out* – life is a living, changing thing – a pattern of ever-changing colours – a symphony of the unpredictable…"

She snorted again, less elegantly this time, "Yes and a bloody inconvenience to the rest of us. People should stay as they are."

"Martin just wanted more," I advocated. I got up and walked about the room.

"Beth, I think we all know what he wanted."

Now she was being coarse but I ignored it.

"But, people *change* – you're not the same person as you were when you met Martin are you?" I entreated.

"Yes I am!" She was quite certain about this too.

"But how old were you then? 22? You've grown since then. You must have changed – got different needs. Different yearnings?"

"No, I *haven't!*" She was cross again, "And I don't see why anyone else has to either! All this 'changing' and 'growing' and 'finding yourself'. What 's the point of it? What are you supposed to do with it when you *do* find it? What would I do if I ever found myself?"

"Scream?" I suggested quietly, then, "I've really no idea."

"I mean," she went on warming to her theme, "have *you* ever felt the need to *'find yourself'*? I hate people who don't stick with their marriage vows, don't you? I'd *hate* to think anyone I know behaved like that. It's what's destroying society! I never thought Martin could do this! How could he do it? Why did he do it?"

"Even educated fleas do it," I suggested quietly, but aloud said, "Yes – Well, do we need to ring and let them know we're on our way – to see these flats?"

"No," she said, "I'm not going. I'm staying here. You've given me an idea."

"I have?" This seemed unlikely.

"Yes," she sounded calmer than she had all afternoon, "I've decided, I don't want to go gallivanting off to a new flat – I'm staying here – get someone to rent a room – that'll pay the mortgage – just until he's back."

She took the suitcase and put it back at the bottom of the stairs.

"Oh right," I said.

There was a pause.

"Thank you for coming around," she said, "you've been a big help." She wasn't being sarcastic either.

"That's okay," I said. It felt like we'd covered a lot of ground in a short time – more than we'd discussed in all the years of dinner parties.

"I'll be off then."

"Thanks. Could you come round again soon? I'll need to know about rent and all that legal stuff?" she said.

"Sure. Glad to help."

Well, it had been better than a magazine and – daytime – telly kind of day anyway.

I took my leave, as they say, but was aware of a yen for more of this adventure and where it may lead. It made a change from the usual routine – plus Angela's circumstances might bring me certain opportunities I had been looking for.

Angela walked me to the door – her dignity restored, I was gratified to note.

"Are you busy tomorrow?" she asked.

As it happened, I was.

"How about Saturday?" I suggested. Saturdays were always a bit on the slow side.

It was agreed we would meet then.

She closed the door behind me and I drove away.

It had been quite a surprising afternoon.

Chapter Two

Saturday rocked up as it generally does without much ado. My life was ticking along as usual only now with the added extra of Angela calling at odd hours needing support – which generally gave me an excuse to leave the TV room and pour a quiet sherry to sip while saying 'Uh-huh' and 'Hmm' at regular intervals into the phone for half an hour whilst filing my nails. She would be thankful and say I was 'the best friend she'd ever had' which, I have to confess, made me feel a bit sad for her as well as a bit anxious for myself.

When I got to Angela's house this Saturday the door was open. Angela called from upstairs when I was hovering on the doorstep, "Hi Beth – I'm up here! Top of the stairs, to the right."

I negotiated my way up the stairs. Angela and Martin were the only people I knew who had pot plants all the way up the stairs – and more than a few of them needed pruning.

The door from which her voice had emanated opened into what seemed to be a dark cave.

This was the newly elected spare room – previously their son's room. Its large television was on, flickering black and white in the darkness.

"Dark in here isn't it?" I said tripping over something in the shadows. "Can I put the light on?"

"It *is* on. Here – have a torch." A bright beam swung towards me out of the gloom. The extra light was enough for me to see that the walls and ceiling were painted black, the carpet was black, the ceiling might have been black but I couldn't see that far to be sure as the torch beam gave up halfway. There was a light on but its lightshade was dark purple and its feeble light had given up long ago. Nearly everything in the room seemed to be black, nearly-black or used to be black.

In the light of the torch I could see that a dustsheet – one of the few exceptions, being a dull grey – lay around some of the floor. Angela was watching the television screen from the room's only chair. She was wearing a big shirt back to front in preparation for painting. Some tins of paint with paint brushes resting on them stood around in the shadows and some of the furniture had been pushed into the centre of the room as if they were going to dance.

"I'm just watching this," she said from the armchair, a tad unnecessarily I thought.

I glanced at the screen.

"Oh yes – that," I said, unenthusiastically.

"My total favourite!" she enthused.

"Another one?" I said, surprised. I had thought that hallowed accolade had already been assigned elsewhere.

"Won't be long," she said reassuringly.

"Right, well – getting on with it I see," I added with a hint of sarcasm.

"Will do! Right after this."

We had agreed on the phone that I'd come round this Saturday morning to lend her a hand in the great task of converting the spare room ready for the influx of tenant and financial solvency. I didn't really want to help her watch old movies. I hadn't seen the outside of a Saturday morning for quite some time after all and I felt my effort should be acknowledged and appreciated.

"I brought some tester pots," I said, raising the bag I was carrying by way of a hint.

"Great!" – the voice was enthusiastic but the eyes never shifted.

"I thought you were going to strip the paper off ready to paint?" – that had been the agreement. "Aren't the tenants due today?"

"Yes, they are, I am. I will. This is just getting to one of the best bits."

As a manager I was used to people jumping up and looking busy when I walked into a room – not slouching deeper into armchairs and sipping coffees without even offering me one. This 'friendship' thing needed more structure, I decided.

"Is there much to do?" I asked, looking around at the black-painted wallpaper – some of it had been pulled off leaving a wide white, diagonal line up one corner. The ripped off part lay in coils in a corner like a sleeping snake.

"Loads! "she said, suddenly animated, "They witnessed the St Valentine's Day Massacre and now they're dressed as women and escaping from the gang but Tony Curtis is in love with…"

"No, I meant the room, not the film!" I think I might have sounded a little impatient at this point, "You know, finding a lodger and all that so you don't have to move house? And the plan? To get Martin back? Save your marriage? You know – Life?"

"I prefer films."

She looked away from the screen – briefly. I think

she might have caught my expression in the torchlight.

"Oh – yes – fine. Okay, I'll put it on pause." She didn't sound pleased.

"Life or the film?" I queried, but she'd pressed the button and the flickering stopped just as Tony's and Marilyn's lips were about to meet.

"Okay… Beth!" she finally rallied to my presence and the world outside the box. "Let's do this! How are you? How's Frank?"

"Oh you know – busy… Golfing… soliciting… I'm off to evening class tonight Life's usual heady round of delights."

She smiled (it was rueful) and sighed heavily, "Alright for some – I suppose," she said. (I think it was 'wistful' she was aiming at.) "Not everyone," she went on," knows what it is to have the love of your life walk out on you and head off to pastures new – leaving you stranded in a middle-aged pool of loneliness!"

She hung her head tragically.

But I was ready for her.

"Oh rubbish!" I responded, "loads of people know. We just have to get on with it. Life isn't about being with people we love. Got the coffee on?"

"Well, don't overwhelm me with care and understanding will you?" She sounded hurt but I didn't bite – some people use 'sounding hurt' as a way of getting what they want and in the time I'd known Angela I'd long decided she was such a one.

"*Everybody* lives in 'pools of loneliness'," I said irritably, "It's a very crowded pool – but at least we can be civilised about it!"

"I'm at the deep end!" she said, equally irritably – which was irritating as *she* was the one irritating *me* and, as such, had no grounds herself for being irritat-ee.

So I said, "And since when was Martin the 'love of your life'? You told me you married him because he had a good job and you wanted kids?"

"Well isn't that the same thing?" she asked.

"Well," I considered, "not in the great romantic works of literature. In which one does the heroine fall into his arms sighing, 'Oh this one'll do – I'm fed up with looking!' Not in the ones I've been to see anyway!"

I prided myself on an intimate knowledge of all the productions of the classics.

"Well," she bridled, "we've been married 20 years that must mean something!"

"Yeh," I was un-impressed, "and you've been bored out of your mind for 19 of them. Like I said – get real and get busy!"

She looked cross, "I've *been* busy – I took your advice about getting active – been gardening like you said – planting wild flowers so it's less work and more modern – digging it over a bit – like you said – had to leave it 'cos of the rain so it's a bit of a mudslide out there now – AND I've decided on yellow for this room 'cos I found two tins of this" –she brandished the tins at me "in the shed or maybe blue 'cos I found these two," she brandished two more, "Under the stairs. But you're right – I felt better doing stuff – making it a better place to be – easier to rent out – And Martin's more likely to come back as well!"

"That's not quite what I meant – I meant do it for *you*… and in case you have to sell it – a nice garden adds thousands!…" I knew this from my sales experience – gardens sold well: I could never think why as they always seemed muddy, messy places to me with insects and things and gardeners are so expensive – but one has to go along with the market of course. I was giving her the benefit of my professional experience at this point but I wasn't charging her for it which I hoped she appreciated, "… and have a nice garden to sit in – so you can enjoy living here – even without Martin and keep it tidy – nothing drags the price of a house down quicker than a runaway garden."

"And it'll help me get a lodger to help with the bills!"

"Exactly… but *tenant*," I corrected, "not lodger. Lodger sounds common, remember?"

"And it won't be for long anyway," she brightened. "Martin will soon be back!"

"You *still* missing him?" I exclaimed. She had been going on about this for an hour or so the other night, as far as I could tell when I'd tuned back into our one-way phone conversation, and I *had* assumed that had been enough on the subject for any lifetime but here she was, off again. I peered around in the gloom for coffee but none was in evidence although there were some biscuits on a plate so there was hope. The service in this friendship was really below par I decided.

"Still?" she pushed her black leatherette-look armchair back into the middle of the room where it almost vanished into its surroundings, "It's only been three weeks!"

"Well," I countered, "you were with him for 20 years – I thought you might be enjoying the change? Most holidays are two weeks – so 'a change as good as a rest' and all that."

Angela had picked up one of the tester pots and she held it, gazing out of the window in a melancholic sort of way, "I even miss our rows," she said.

"Here – have a biccie," I said, throwing protocol to the winds in desperation and taking one myself, "What did you row about?"

She sighed nostalgically, and bit her biscuit, "Oh the usual, you know..." she waved the biscuit in a vague arc…," housework, meals, work, money, Hugo, parenting styles, my car, his car, hobbies and, of course, politics; relatives, people we know, the telly…" She paused for breath.

"That's quite a list," I commented. I had, after all, only ever witnessed them together at dinner parties and cocktail 'do's' discussing wine, their latest holiday and furnishing plans in polite, modulated tones along with everybody else.

"Well," Angie said, defensively, "*all* couples have rows."

"Yeh," I had to concede, "but most do other things besides."

"So what do you and Frank row about?" was her next question, loading a brush from a tester pot and dabbing it gingerly on the wall.

"We don't," I answered, truthfully.

"Golly!" she looked at me, impressed. "You and Frank must be really compatible!"

"Not really," I had to disillusion her. "We just hardly ever see each other. Works like a dream. What do you think of that yellow?"

She squinted at the oblong patch she had painted on the wall.

"Bit bright?" she ventured.

"I think it might damage someone's retinas.

Permanently. They could sue."

I read the side of the pot, "'Pale Primrose' it says here."

"Same old story," she said, like somebody very old and wise, 'That's what it says on the tin – 'Pale Primrose' – as it blinds you like a nuclear bomb going off. It's like that with people isn't it – never *in* side the tin what it says on the *out* side."

I allowed her that – most of my life depended on the truth of it after all. Imagine a world where we all went around being honest and open with each other? I suppressed a shudder.

She went on, "And like adverts – like that picture showing those people and their dog – all happily decorating a room together."

"Yes?" I hadn't seen it.

"There they all are – perfectly painted room – all smiles, spotless clothes everybody pristine – even the dog! Me and Martin – yes, okay, Martin and me – I mean if we did any painting – I ended up looking like I'd been tie-dyed, Martin would have stepped in the tin at least twice, half the paint would be on the carpet and we wouldn't be on speaking terms for a week."

She held up her yellow streaked hand and sleeve as evidence. There was more paint on either of them than on the patch on the wall.

"Just as well you never had a dog?" I suggested, brightly.

"Martin's allergic." She went quiet and looked anxious. "Beth," she looked at me, "am I taking on too much – re-decorating? Without Martin? We did the house together. Eventually. Took us years. Should I just get in a painter and decorator?"

She was looking threateningly sentimental and flimsy again.

"You can't afford that," I said practically. "You need a lodger – until Martin gets back. You can't rent out a tip of a room with black walls – you can't afford to pay someone so, yes, you need to do it – but I'm here to help – How about this?" I dug out one of the tester pots, "A peachy kind of orange – you like oranges – it's a dark room – it needs a bright colour – brightens up the corners lovely, loses the shadows, hides the dark patches?"

She spotted the flaw. "But it leaves glowing blotches all over the floor. You can't get them off you know: When me and Martin – sorry, yes, Martin and me – okay – Martin *and I*… were decorating – I made a little tiny spot – tried to get it off – two hours later it was a stain a mile wide all over the living room carpet. That's why we got the piano. Can't play the thing but what else can you put in the middle of a room?"

"I did wonder why you have a piano there. I

thought it was a cherished antique and that you and Martin did duets of an evening."

"That was just a cover story – it's just hiding a paint stain."

I felt so disillusioned. It had been such a romantic image.

"And then," Angela went on, "I stepped in a little wet paint – spot – I didn't notice until I had a dotted line all the way to the bathroom and back… on a russet carpet!"

She seemed depressed at this unhappy memory.

"Is that why…?"

"Yes, *that's* why we had those little mats put all the way down the hallway with potted plants and all the way up the stairs. They're tricky to get past but they *do* cover all the stains."

"Oh," I said. (Honestly, you think you know someone!) "But you said you were doing your bit to replace the Amazon -that time when I tripped over that rubber plant and fell down the stairs."

"Yes, that's what we *tell* people," she protested, all wide eyed and innocent. "Well, you feel so silly, don't you, telling people you trod in some paint and stomped it all the way to the toilet?"

I had to agree.

I looked around, wondering what other secrets the

well-presented house was holding.

"Well, I won't do that again," she said cheerfully, "It's only one room we're painting after all – just for the lodger."

"Tenant," I corrected her, patiently.

"Tenant. What other testers did you get?"

"This nice turquoise. And a nice quiet grey. A subtle pink. There's quite a choice…"

"Is this such a good idea though Beth?" she was holding the yellowed paint brush and was looking at it in what looked like despair, "Can't I just go on holiday and when I come back everything will be back to normal. I just want to be back to normal. Martin here – me here – this room empty – Hugo on his way to visit – the telly on."

I rallied her, "Come *on*, I know it's difficult. It's early days yet-but this'll look *great* when you've finished and got everything back in place. I'll help. And it won't be for long," I added (I thought the moment seemed to call for a touch of denial.).

"It won't be will it!" she said more cheerfully. "Martin and Allan will split up and Martin will be back! But," she looked solemn again, "it'll be weird having a stranger, the tenant, in the house in the meantime. In *our* house."

She looked fragile again.

This was getting to be hard work.

"Strangers are only friends you haven't met yet," I offered, trying not to wince at the exhausted platitude which I'd read on so many plaques in the homes of the kind of person who said that kind of thing without wincing – which I only ever visited because I had to professionally when they had decided to sell their house and wanted an estate agent's advice. Taking those plaques off the wall was usually among the first such advice I generally offered.

She frowned. "Was that from one of your self-help books?"

"Yes," I lied, "my favourite – *'A Platitude a Day Keeps Reality Away'*. Works a treat for me."

"I've thought of writing a self-help book – they're so helpful!" she said enthusiastically.

"Good idea – you could make a million! They do – lot of people need help out there. I've met a lot of them."

"I could help them!" Angela was inspired and didn't notice the flecks of yellow flying off her brandished paintbrush into the dark as she seized on the idea.

"You could! It's an idea. There are a lot of such books out there as well though. You'd need a good punchy title – so yours would stand out," I advised.

"I've got one," she said, rubbing at the spattered

wall with her sleeve, "How about, '*How to Totally Enhance Your Life and Reach A Higher Harmonious Inner Being*'. What do you think?"

I pulled a face. "Bit long. How about, '*Coping with Crap – for Beginners*'?"

She pondered, shaking her head. "Not sure I could write that. I don't know how to… cope with crap. Anyway," she brightened. "I prefer the books that just get you to look the other way and – *kapow*! the 'crap' – although I *do* prefer the word 'problem' – just isn't there anymore – it's all in your *mind*. Much more relaxing! Most problems go away if you look at them differently, or don't look at them at all, you see?"

"Sounds good," I agreed, "but let's get this lodger in place first so you can at least pay the bills while you're writing the international best seller. Court summons hardly ever go away when you look at them differently… I've tried. Or, you know," I said, returning to a theme, "you *could* make Martin pay the mortgage as he's the one who's left?"

"He hasn't *left* – he's just having a few weeks away – okay, a couple of months maximum. He'll be back! This marriage is not *over*. Him and Allan are going to split up any day now and he'll be back." (She should of course have said 'He and Allan' but I magnanimously let it pass.)

"Of course," I said, "I forget sometimes. Is this

the room you're going to rent out?" I considered the dinner plate sized, yellow stain she had so far painted on one wall.

"Yes... It's Hugo's."

"I know – but he'll be visiting won't he?"

"Yeh, no problem."

"But he visits nearly every year! Where's he going to sleep?"

"No problem – he's not due for months and it'll all be back to normal by then – just a quick lick of black paint and his room is back."

I noticed she was looking furtive.

"Have you *told* Hugo what's happened?" I asked, suspiciously.

"No, of course not!" she insisted, "Nothing to tell! Martin will be back before his next visit –so he need never know. Hugo's happy in his life over in Canada – why upset him?"

"Er, but what if…" I began thinking it was time somebody mentioned the unmentionable but I didn't get far...

"So – where shall we start?" she said, loudly and brusquely, cutting across me and my 'what if'. "I think we should go with the blue. I read somewhere that people with yellow rooms commit suicide, Here." She stepped to the window and pulled open the black curtains. My eyes protested at the blinding dazzle after all the dark.

"No, no," I said, "that was just to show how one thing doesn't necessarily cause another just because they are both present: some people commit suicide – some of them have yellow kitchens – it was about statistics – it doesn't mean having a yellow kitchen *makes* you commit suicide. You know?"

She looked at me blankly.

"It's how newspapers work – they report two things and pretend one caused…" she looked at me even more blankly. I let it go. I'd enjoyed Sociology 101 but had dropped it for the unit in High Finance in Housing. "So… painting the room… shall we?" I said.

She looked around, "It looks worse in daylight – I'll have to get a new carpet."

"No you won't!" My estate agent and High Finance instincts kicked in, "No need for a new carpet! Too expensive – just move the furniture about – cover up the worn patches and stains here and there. You'd never tell. It's only for a lodger."

"Tenant," she said, a bit pedantically, I thought. "Do you think so? I can't put a piano in every room."

"Sure – here – let me… there." I'd had plenty of practice at making rooms look nicer, bigger, worth more – by moving furniture about – for years," Just move this here – put that there – Simple. Put that rug there – move this chair… there… you can't see it now. Put that chair there – nobody will notice. And push the bed across… great! As long as they move around quite a lot – and don't look at any one place for too long – they'll never notice!"

"Ok," she looked impressed, "I'll rent it out to someone who's hyperactive, short-sighted and with no curiosity. Gosh, you are strong! I could never have lifted that. But is it okay to have the bed in the middle of the room?"

"Sure. Of course it is. Just call it a futon."

"Cool! Sounds trendy! And I expect the lodger'll want to bring their own stuff and furniture. That will fill the room."

"Tenant," I reminded her again, "but they probably won't *have* any stuff – people looking for a room – probably not well off. First time away from home I expect, or someone else going through divorce."

"I'm not *going* through a divorce. And I only want somebody nice. Not just anybody."

"But of course they won't be *nice* – they're not well – off. No-one's nice if they're not well off – we know that. Probably won't be *our* kind of people at all. Probably unemployed. But they're just here to pay the mortgage remember. For now!"

"They?" she looked horrified.

"No I meant – he! Or she! Not they!"

"And I don't *want* anyone unemployed – hanging around all day!"

"They'd be in their room."

"Yes but I'd know they were *there*," she whispered.

"Well yes, they'd be there. And you'd be at work all week," I pointed out.

"But they'd be here. I'd *know* they were here. In our house – breathing!"

"Well you *do* want someone who breathes. Don't want zombies and the un-dead wandering about, do we? Mind you," I muttered, remembering Martin, "whatever you're used to. But I shouldn't worry, unemployed folk are fully employed all day these days; being interviewed about *why* they're unemployed and filling in forms proving they *are* unemployed and going to interviews miles away for jobs they can't get to on time to do – and going to more interviews about why their money's been cut off again when they didn't fill the forms in on time because they had to go to an interview. It's a busy life being unemployed-you'd probably never see them, it'll be fine."

She didn't look convinced, "Hmm. Well if you're sure. But – if they get their money cut off they won't be able to pay me my rent?"

"No problem," I assured her, cheerfully. "Just chuck them out and get another one – there'll be plenty of them about now that Clancy's in town has closed – they employed hundreds they did. They'll all be looking for somewhere cheaper to live. You could even put the rent up." I was always one to spot the silver lining.

"Well, if you're sure."

"Of course I'm sure. Not straightaway though. Having somebody unemployed would be good – you could get them to do some housework in exchange for food."

"Oh that sounds good!" she sounded more positive now.

"And don't you drop your standards – just be clear from the start – this is still *your* house – they just live in *this* room. They can use the kitchen and the facilities – maybe you can give them time slots – but that's all. And the money will pay the mortgage – or most of it. C'mon – you decided this is the best plan."

"Did I?"

"Well somebody did. And it wasn't me. My idea was to make Martin pay, Yes, of *course* you did. We've done very well," (we had got as far as deciding on the colour of the paint after all). "Let's have a break. Coffee?"

We left the cave and went downstairs.

"Speaking of breaks," Angela said, wandering into the kitchen and fetching down the cups (I hadn't often been into these more intimate areas of the house before so I had a good look around. It was fairly clean but obviously lacked the weekly input of a professional which I find so necessary for my own standards), "I broke three ornaments moving about in Hugo's room in the dark before I found the lamp," she confessed.

"Were they Hugo's?" I queried. Her son wasn't one for ornaments to my recollection. Bongs, yes, but ornamental items in his room – not so much. "Valuable?"

"No – they were mine – ours I mean – I hid them- I mean put them in there after Hugo left home – They were presents from Martin's mum – hideous things – I'll have to replace them before Martin gets back."

"Why?"

Presents from his mum," she said a bit louder – as if my query had arisen from my not having heard this vital point, which it hadn't. "Though I'm convinced they were bought just to give me something else to dust. Nasty little ornaments! Part of her plan to make me the perfect little housewife – for her perfect little prince!" She sounded quite bitter at this point.

"So," I decided it was time to move on, "how's his mum taking to her 'perfect prince's' new tangent in life? I know she never thought you were a good enough woman for her son – but at least you *are* a woman. Wonder if she's met Allan yet?"

Angela sipped her coffee. "I expect she'll be pleased. It's quite trendy now to have a gay child. Even temporarily gay like this is. I expect her and Allan will get on like a house on fire – I never managed to get on her right side somehow. She was always telling me how to do my hair."

"At least you've got hair. Allan hasn't much has he? That should make her happy."

She shook her head, "That won't get him off the hook – he has some – she'll try and make him do that thing, you know, grow his side bits and plait it across his forehead, you'll see. She was forever telling me what to wear or dropping hints how to 'improve my figure'. Buying me clothes she liked and expecting me to wear them."

"Well, maybe she never had a Barbie doll when she was a kid and she was trying to catch up?" I offered.

"Martin said I had a complex. I think she gave me one."

"Well he's the psychiatrist," I pointed out. "With that lot, psychiatrists and all them, whenever someone's got a problem it's because they have a *complex*. It's never because they've actually got a problem."

"True – I always thought it was because I was too polite or too scared to tell her to get knotted – probably 'cos I 'have a complex'."

"Well, now she's got a Ken instead of a Barbie... Wonder if she'll do the same routine with him?"

"Yes, of course! She'll make his paunch her personal crusade. She was always trying to get me to lose weight. But if she drives Allan away with all her pestering and snide remarks Martin will be back here all the quicker!"

"You do still want him back?" I asked.

But she was in full flood speculating, "But on the other hand she might enjoy the new project. And Allan might enjoy being fussed over! She might *not* have met him though – they've been seeing each other for three years and kept it secret from me so no doubt from her too."

"Three years? Allan and Martin?"

"Yeh, Martin spilled the beans to me before he left. Said he'd been wanting to tell me but … you know. He said him and Allan had split up several times during those years but always got back together. He said they always practised safe sex so I had no worries there – which was nice."

"Yes, that's something – nothing like dying of the clap like in the good old days Our great grandmothers did without knowing where it came from, but at least they died helping one of the biggest industries of the day," I mused, I had enjoyed the evening classes on Victorian history too although I hadn't finished the course. "Well that's one worry less anyway. But three years is a bit serious though isn't it? Have you had any flings in that time?"

Her glare at me answered that one.

"Well, sauce for the goose..." I muttered, turning my back and quietly tipping the remnants of a truly awful cup of coffee quietly down the sink and looking around for the biscuits.

"I'm not *that* sort of woman!" she declared, "I'll have to go online and look around," she continued.

"That's more like it!" I approved – "get yourself a toy boy!" (One that can make decent coffee I wanted to add but didn't.)

She was glaring again. "No – I *meant* to find replacements for the ornaments. Martin and his mum are bound to notice if I don't – she comes around at Christmas and he always puts them on display when she's here to make it look as if we like them and don't hide them in Hugo's room the rest of the year!"

Why on Earth, I wondered, did she want to keep being part of such an awful family? Cut and run for the hills, I thought – but didn't say.

"Do you think she'll still be coming around at Christmas?" I asked.

"Of course – this will all be over by then…"

"Er… Haven't we heard that phrase somewhere before?"

"…*and*," Angela went on, ignoring my interruption, "even if it isn't, she will have forgiven him whether he tells her about it or not – he's still her little prince. She'll forgive him anything when she knows what their new postcode is – very upmarket – much better than here."

"How come – is he rich? *Are* accountants rich?"

This was news to me.

"The crooked ones are. Allan inherited, Martin said – his dad left him a bundle."

"So he was able to move out and buy a flat with Martin?" I noted. That was two commissions I'd missed so far, I thought. "Rich, eh? Well that must add to the attraction – paunch and bald patch or no."

I liked rich men myself. I'd even married one.

"Yes," she said angrily, "tempting my Martin away with his money – his flash lifestyle – his glittering baubles…"

"Has he got…?"

"I meant his jewellery – fancy watch and rings and

flash car as well, I bet."

"Right, of course."

"And Martin's mum would love all that of course. She always wanted her son to move up in the world – thought I was holding him back. I think pink would be better than yellow – people like pink better than yellow."

"Nonsense," I said, "people like yellow. I've sold loads of houses which were yellow – people think it's 'sunny'."

"Then why do they commit suicide?"

"They don't –that was just…" I let it go again.

"Anyway, I'm not selling – just having someone in to pay the mortgage for a while… Just," and I joined in at this point to repeat the already well-worn phrase…" until Martin gets back."

She didn't catch my tone of irony.

"Yeh, about them splitting up," I asked, taking another biccie, "any news on that front?"

"I saw them yesterday – at work in the lunch break in the canteen," she answered.

"So they're back from their honey… I mean, holiday… anyway."

"Yes," she said sadly, "and still together… I hoped it would split them up – going on holiday – me and

Martin would always ended up having rows on holidays... alright, Martin and I... but they were eating soup in the canteen and chatting. I couldn't hear what they were chatting about. I did sneak up but the giant, cardboard cut-out advert for ice-cream I was hidden behind fell over. I had to pretend I was interested in what kind of ice-cream it was and bought a pot. It was horrible. Pistachio."

"Ah," I nodded sympathetically – as one who knew what it was to bite into disappointing ice-cream.

She shook her head at the memory, "I mean who'd put pistachio in ice cream?"

I asked, "How did you feel after that?"

"A bit sick," she said, "wish I'd just gone with the strawberry."

"No, I meant how did you feel after seeing them together."

"Oh right," she sighed. "Not great. Martin's growing a beard again and his taste in shirts is definitely showing signs of deterioration. I always bought his shirts for him."

She relapsed into staring into her coffee cup. It was time for more work.

"I've been thinking," I announced. "You must get a new job."

She looked up, alarmed.

"It won't do you any good seeing them every day – it's no good you all working in the same place. Did they see you?"

She frowned, remembering. "Probably – I think half the canteen did – A bit silly; falling over a cardboard ice-cream – grazed my shin. Stupid place anyway to put a cardboard ice-cream…"

"And after that?" (This really *was* hard work. I resisted asking where a sensible place would be to put a cardboard ice-cream as it felt like a tangent in which we could become totally lost.)

"Well," she re-focused, "Martin was all tanned and with his wrist in plaster. That'll teach him to go skiing. Allan seemed unscathed – more's the pity… We didn't speak – Martin just made an awkward nod at me across the canteen."

I speculated, "There's much might be contained in an awkward nod. That's as much as you could expect at this stage."

This did not cheer her. "Well, not really," she said, looking at the eye-level steam extractor with an agonised expression, "I had been rather hoping that, on seeing me, he'd realise his terrible mistake and come running back – begging me to forgive him – and we'd have a passionate embrace in the middle of the canteen with everyone watching and cheering. No cardboard ice cream at all."

It was a beautiful vision.

"… And pistachio all over your face as the credits roll – You really do watch a lot of films don't you? Well, at least an awkward nod sounds friendly. You can't always gauge passion in a nod."

"Thought I'd be better after all these weeks. Thought I'd be cool but I just got all muddled and asked for cabbage with my bolognaise," she recalled.

"I've often wondered what that would be like," I pondered.

"I wouldn't recommend it!" She was quite decisive on this point.

"Makes sense," I nodded, "if it did work I'm sure 'cabbage a la bolognaise' would be a thing."

I sighed in empathy, thinking of her ordeal of seeing her husband with his new love. "Must have been a shock for you the first time," I said sympathetically, "but it should get better after a while."

"No I don't think I'll try it again. I'll stick with spaghetti." She shook her head emphatically.

"No," I explained, "I meant seeing Martin and Allan together."

"Oh right, yes. But I'm going to get him back though. Twenty years of marriage must count for something!"

"Of course, yes. Minus the three years they've

been seeing each other on the quiet – that's 17 years."

She sounded quite abrupt. "Yes – Thanks Beth- you always *were* good at maths. And where's Frank today?"

"Golf. Weekends are for golf. Weekdays for work. Well, Angie, I've come to be helpful – shall we get on?"

"Oh thanks –yes."

Coffee cups were put in the sink and we went back up to the cave. "Spare overalls are on the stepladder. What do you think of this border?" She pulled open a narrow roll of wallpaper.

I pulled a face, "Bit insipid?"

"Oh." She looked crestfallen, I think is the word – although she'd never had a crest.

I rushed to back-pedal, I think is the term – although I wasn't on a bicycle.

"But insipid in a *nice* way," I assured her, "– insipid is all the rage this year. Insipid is the new black!"

She was reassured. "Yes – I chose it to be nice and quiet – for a nice quiet person – in a nice quiet room."

"That's what they say about mass murderers isn't it – *'they always seemed so nice and quiet'*. If I ever wanted to get away with a murder I'd act like a loudmouthed, screaming banshee. The police wouldn't look at me twice."

Her face fell. "Thanks for that happy thought, about murder, just as I'm about to invite a complete stranger to live in my house!"

"Don't worry!" I reassured her, "strangers are quite safe – you're more likely to get murdered by your husband than anyone else so statistically you're actually much safer now that Martin has moved out – look at it that way!"

A perfectly sound point I thought – but she had to be awkward, "I don't *want* to look at it that way – Martin *isn't* a murderer!"

I'd put on the overalls and took a brush and a pot of paint up to the top of the stepladder, "I always *did* wonder what you saw in him. But that's a pretty low bar I have to say! And nobody ever is a murderer – until they murder somebody!"

She was insistent, "He wouldn't murder anybody!"

She was sticking to her guns. "He's a very *well* qualified psychologist, Beth! Very well qualified psychologists don't murder other people… usually."

"Anyway." (I'd opened my mouth to object at this point but she raised her hand to silence me.)

"And I don't like the house being empty – it doesn't feel safe at all. I do miss him being here – this is just a temporary measure having a lodger."

"Tenant."

"Whatever. I do miss him."

"What do you miss?" I stroked a line of yellow paint over the black. I was reminded of wasps.

"Oh you know," she was at the other wall, in the big shirt, dabbing pink, "it's the little things – little squabbles over whose turn it is with the remote. Having someone there to wipe as you wash. Someone coming home and telling you what a rotten day they've had – and listening to what a rotten day you've had."

"Ah – the stuff of dreams!" I commented.

"And I am hoping to get a mature student – who's not a murderer."

"Did you put that in the advert?"

"No – do you think I should have done?"

"No, I think some things are just understood. Any responses yet?"

"Four. I'm trying to get this room ready before they come round but left it a bit late.. I thought I'd rather they called when you were here if that's okay – back me up a bit?"

"Great – just give me the nod at the ones you don't like and I'll heave them out the door. What do you think?"

I invited her to look at the square foot I'd daubed.

She looked at it and at her own effort.

"I suppose I could just economise –get rid of the car – travel by bus?"

"Angie – we're not living in the Dark Ages. You're supposed to be starting out as wild, young-ish and free – you can't be very wild *or* free stuck at a bus stop."

"Or I could switch supermarkets and give up luxuries?"

This was serious. "Switch supermarkets? You don't mean…?"

I was aghast.

"Well I have to economise!" she exclaimed, defensively.

"Yes, but I *do* hope we'll still be able to be friends!"

"Just a *few* changes."

"But no need for extremes!" I felt an intervention was necessary at this point.

"I mean people might see you if you went… *there*. And they *know* you know me! And everyone needs a car! Everyone *I* know anyway. Or would *want* to know," I said, emphasising this last phrase quite pointedly.

"There *must* be a way," she sounded desperate. "When I go on holidays I love walking around the little villages. So why can't I walk around here?"

I thought for a moment. "Because: here it never

stops raining; you're half a mile from the nearest bus stop; this isn't a 'pretty little village' the nearest shops are three and a half miles away – you'd starve to death in a week."

She rejoined the affray, "I'll shop online – they deliver to your door. I've got a freezer – only need to shop once a month. Take a packed lunch to work – save a fortune!"

"But," I said, seeing that she just didn't understand, "we're *not* that sort of people! The neighbours would see the van for crying out loud! And without a car..." I looked around for another image, "you'll lose all the *spontaneity* of life – all the last-minute decisions to rush out of the door into new adventure – all care to the wind and unknown horizons...!"

"I've got a Fiesta, Beth, not a helicopter. And the last time I ran out of the door was when my pink – bag blew in the road. Plastic milk bottles scattered across the neighbourhood. I don't really *do* spontaneity."

I insisted, "You must do more in future. Build it in. Decide. Do spontaneity! Be wild!"

I brandished my paintbrush. A globule of yellow slid off it and landed just outside the remit of the dustsheet.

"Okay, "she shrugged, carrying on with painting a pink square, "I'll put it on my To Do list. 'Be Spontaneous. Do Wild.' I have drawn up a tenant's contract, like you said, I think it covers everything, and made an Inventory – two copies."

"Good – can't be too careful. Make sure you haven't missed anything and get them to sign it. They might be part of a gang. Removal van outside – you're out at work – you come back to bare floorboards and empty curtain rails!"

"I could just forget about having a tenant and live on beans for a few months?"

But that wouldn't do at all, I thought, I had my own plans after all.

"No! You're going to *enjoy* this new life! I mean – this new six months! You mustn't sink into penury and desperation. Nothing attractive about squalor – except in an oil painting."

"But strangers can be difficult to live with!"

"Strangers are *supposed* to be difficult – But look on the bright side – most people are murdered by someone they know not by strangers, did you know that?"

"Could you stop going on about murder?"

I considered, "Most people get murdered by someone they know. So… if you know a lot of people I suppose the chances increase – that one of them is a murderer and will murder you?"

"So… best not to know many people I suppose?"

"Yes… but mostly it's people you're related to who are the danger – and you can't un-know your relatives or your partner can you?"

"Suppose."

"So… people who don't know anybody'd be quite safe. If it's someone you know who usually murders you – and you don't know anybody – then there's no problem."

"So the quiet lonely ones with no friends are the safest?"

"Yes, that's it!" I agreed, "It's all the sociable types, going out, having friends, getting married – they're the ones most likely to get bumped off!"

"Oh dear!"

Her hand went to her throat.

I had another thought, "Maybe it's affecting evolution – if we're more likely to survive – if we live alone and stay home all the time – then gradually we'll evolve into a species which stays home every night and has no friends? I think we're half way there."

"Survival of the loneliest?" said Angela. "So… best way to avoid being murdered is to lurk in your bedsit on your own. That's a plan!" she brightened.

"Yes," I concluded, "and murder someone yourself! Statistically that would probably make you immune. How many murderers get murdered? Hardly any I bet!"

At this happy thought there was a knock on the door.

Angela jumped a little.

"Someone's knocking?" she pointed out. She looked at the door but it didn't do anything.

"Shall I get it?" I suggested.

A voice floated up the stairs.

"Halloo? Shall I come up Sorry I'm a bit early."

"Come on up!" I called, as Angela seemed transfixed.

A younger woman in smart casuals arrived in our midst.

"Hello!"

We all said our hellos. Angela looked at me as if she wanted me to take the lead but I felt as the hostess and homeowner she really needed to assert herself here.

So I said, "Oh hi, do come in I'll go and put kettle on," and made my exit.

I didn't mind helping Angela but I didn't want to carry her.

"Hi, yes, are you on your own?" I heard Angela ask, I left the door open to listen, "We were just talking about murder." Angela said in a friendly way, as I left.

"Oh! Ah!" said her young visitor.

"Yes," Angela went on, "about how it's the quiet ones you have to look out for – and people you know." I stopped halfway down the stairs and considered whether to return – but I carried on, put the kettle on and listened from the kitchen door.

"Oh Right! This is, er, nice," the potential tenant was saying.

"Which of those colours would you like it to be?" Angie ploughed on," We're just re-doing it. It isn't going to be suicide yellow that's for sure. Had enough of that!"

There was a mumbled response to this. I thought Angie would probably get off the subject of murder and suicide quite soon.

"Yes, we want to cover up the dark patches and the shadows and stains." She added helpfully, in case the tenant hadn't noticed these.

"Oh – yes – good – has your last tenant been gone long?" the visitor asked.

"O it wasn't a tenant dear – it was my husband – but he's gone to a better place now. I don't want to talk about it."

"Oh, I'm sorry!"

"But it's not over yet," said Angie, "– he'll be back – you can be sure of that."

"Oh really?"

"Yes, I still see him now and again. And I don't think he's happy."

"O dear!"

"He was very quiet usually. Like me. Are you quiet?"

"Oh, er, quite quiet. Not extremely so. Average really. Averagely quiet. Is quiet good?"

"I do like a quiet house. It's much quieter now he's gone."

"Oh right! Nice view. Is that the garden?"

"Yes but you don't want to look at the garden – it's still all dug over and in a mess. Had to do a lot of digging. I've only just finished covering it all over."

"Oh right!"

"Yes it was the best I could do for him. And me of course. It'll be alright in the Spring – it'll look quite natural then when the flowers come up. Beth's idea."

"Was it? You and… I didn't catch her name?"

"Beth? I'm Angela, she's been a great help to me just lately. Covering up in here and everything. Giving me a few tips. You need two people for some jobs don't you? And she's much stronger than she looks."

"Oh, is she?"

"Her husband's still around – they get on alright though so the same thing probably won't happen there."

"Oh good!"

"Yes. So this is all new to me – Quite exciting. A whole new me! I'm redecorating this room but keeping the rest of the house just as he liked it for when he comes back."

"Is that often?"

"Oh I'm sure you'll see him before too long."

I stuck the mugs on the tray and headed up the stairs.

"O right – well – thanks" I heard our visitor say, "I've got a few other places to look at so I'd best be on my way!"

"Oh you mustn't go!" I heard Angela cry.

"Oh please… I'm only 23…!"

I had arrived in the doorway with the tray. Beth had her back to me and was standing between the visitor and the door who was looking over her shoulder at me, panic stricken.

Then she suddenly pushed past Angela and me and headed down the stairs. Two of the coffee mugs spilled onto the tray as she pushed passed saying, "O sorry – No, yes, it's very nice, no, let me out! I'm just a bit late. No don't worry I'll see myself out. Bye. Thank you."

We watched her go.

"That was a bit rude!" said Angela, quietly.

Our visitor looked over her shoulder a few times before she reached the front door and almost ran through it.

"Bye!" Angela called after her. "Do call back soon!" She took a coffee and wiped the spill off the side with her hand, "Well that went well. Wonder if she'll be back?"

"I shouldn't think so by the look on her face. What were you talking to her about?" I didn't like to admit I'd been eavesdropping.

"Nothing much – just small talk really. I should have gone with pink – pink's warmer. Let's change it to pink."

"Yes, maybe. It'll be better when the curtains are back up, furniture in, pictures on the wall. It'll be fine. Here. May as well drink this."

"You ever been a lodger? A tenant?" she asked.

We sat on the dustsheets with our three coffees.

"No, but I've been married to Frank – amounts to the same thing. Getting in someone else's way in a confined space and sharing the bills."

"Sounds good!"

"It is. Everything works well – until you get to the

kitchen and the bathroom. If we didn't have those two rooms life would be much sweeter and there would be no more wars." I took a biccie.

"Why? What happens in bathrooms and kitchens?"

"The trouble always starts there. There are nearly seven billion people on this planet and no two of them have anything like the same idea about where toothbrushes go. Or flannels!"

"Is that bad?"

"Lethal! Or where towels belong or where cutlery needs to be or how long you can leave dishes 'in soak' or what a 'clean bath' actually *is* or where to hang washing."

"Sounds tricky."

"Too true. The United Nations could have got it sorted the first day it was formed but, no, they missed their chance – wasted their time on trivial issues like famine and weapons deployment. Left us all to flounder and fall out over the real issues in life – like 'who put their socks there?' Or, how many pairs of shoes can go in a hallway before it can be called 'a mess' – Did you know some people actually think having an interesting collection of shoes is 'over indulgent' and they want them put away in cupboards! I mean what's the point of having piles of designer shoes if you bung them in cupboards where no one can see them? Any fool knows you need to let them stay 'on display' so others can enjoy. Sorry, this isn't about me – it's about you. What were we talking about?"

I wondered if I'd said too much.

"Being in kitchens or bathrooms?"

"Or hallways. I forgot hallway – hallways are lethal too. If they built houses without bathrooms, kitchens or hallways we'd all be fine, live longer and the divorce courts could close."

"Maybe when I get a tenant I should ask her to leave her shoes on and stay in her room?"

"Yes! Good idea – she could have a commode and never come out. That would work. It's all about territory. How territorial are you?"

She shrugged, "Never thought about it."

"Well, do you mind other people using your favourite coffee mug at work, for instance?"

"O god, no! I don't speak to people if they do that."

"Do you tell them what they've done wrong first, before you freeze them out?"

"No! Why should I? They should work that out for themselves. But I sometimes drop things on their desk as a hint."

"Hm! So... you don't communicate your anger?

Did Martin ever do anything which got on your nerves?" I enquired.

"Oh no – nothing, well, not much," she was clear about this.

I waited.

"Hardly anything. Not at all. Snoring was bad," she went on.

"So he kept you awake?" I prompted.

"No, so he slept in the spare room."

"Oh – so that wasn't so bad then."

"… and he'd drink milk…"

"In the spare room?"

"No – straight from the carton."

"Oh my god!" I had heard rumours of such things but hadn't believed them.

"He said there were only the two of us, once Hugo left home, so it didn't matter. He always drank from the carton. So I'd always get a carton of UHT for me – He hated UHT milk. So do I – but at least it was clean."

"That sounds difficult."

"Not as bad as him eating."

"Really? He ate too?"

"I don't know how he did it really. It would start

off quite innocently, just a slight slurp as he put the first forkful in his mouth."

"Yes?" I was all ears.

"Then you'd be lulled into a false sense of security as he began to chew. Side to side."

"Side to side? Like a …?"

"Yes – like a camel. Then his tongue would start to get in on the act – pushing it about inside and he'd park it in his cheek while he chewed on the tough bits and then he'd have to open up a bit to get air so his lips would smack as his teeth were grinding and his cheeks were making odd hollow noises like a bass rhythm section."

"Oh dear."

"Once he'd really got going it sounded like the food was fighting to get out of his mouth and back on the plate but he would just carry on – torturing it to death."

"Right."

"And then he'd swallow."

"That would be better then."

"And him swallowing sounded like someone pulling a toilet plunger out of a muddy swamp… or out of a toilet."

"Oh!"

"And then it would start again – with another forkful." She had gone into a sort of trance at this point.

"Ah!" I was lost for words.

"And then it would go on. And on. Until the last mouthful. You wouldn't believe it if you weren't there to hear it."

"I wondered why you always had loud music playing when we came round for dinner. And you never came to ours. Always some excuse. Did you eat out often?"

"As often as possible – I always wanted to go to nice noisy places where there was plenty of other racket going on so I didn't have to listen to it. But he liked quiet little places. At least they were quiet until he got started. He could clear a room inside two courses. I think places would have paid for us to stay away. I used to put the radio on when we were home to drown the worst of it."

"So you're not missing that aspect of the relationship then? There's always *some* things about a relationship which don't work *so* well... helps us when that relationship come to..." but she hadn't finished.

"That was nothing compared to what he did in the bathroom."

"God! What did he do in there?"

"He'd always leave a ring. Always. Just a ring. Just the one."

"On the bath?"

"Yes of course on the bath – where else?"

Well I didn't like to say, being delicately bred.

"That is annoying. He didn't know how to clean a bath?"

"Apparently not. His mother had always done it for him of course. Her 'little prince'. I used to clean it off – but then I stopped. And I'd leave them there. Eventually you could have counted them – the rings."

"To see how old the bath was?"

"No that's trees. And I'd leave my ring too – I'd make sure it was shallower than his so it didn't blur the issue. I had baths always the exact same depth and just a bit shallower than his – just to be clear."

"Got quite intense then, this bath thing?"

She didn't pause.

"But he didn't get the hint. Don't think he even noticed. Eventually the rings all joined up."

"Right. Gosh, look at the time! Isn't it amazing what you find out about somebody in casual conversation?"

"I switched to using the shower," she went on.

"Did you not talk about it?"

"No – we're not the talking sort. I don't like yakking on about things."

"Yeh I've noticed that. Right. Have you thought about this tenancy idea – do you think it's right for you? Really? Maybe moving to a flat…"

"Did you ever have these problems with Frank – the ring in the bath and so on?"

"Hell no, we got a cleaner – let her sort it out! Still, every marriage…"

"And then there was the breathing…"

"The breathing? He breathed as well?" There seemed no way out. I took the other cupful of lukewarm coffee and resigned myself. My own marriage was boring, never mind other people's, but you have to, don't you – for a friend?

"In front of the telly, sitting there, mug in hand and then the wind would start – whistling through his nostrils – one at a time I think. In out, in out."

"I get the picture," I reassured her earnestly.

"And do you know what the worst was?"

"The worst thing about this marriage?"

"Yes, it was pointless."

"Well, that's a bit harsh, some people think marriage is outmoded but others…"

"No! *Pointless*! The game show. He'd watch it and

snap out all the answers he knew as quick as he could. And if anyone got an answer wrong he'd snort down his nose and say 'what an idiot' Every time. Every single time. Even if it was an answer he didn't know. And then go back to breathing. He got all excited if the questions were about geography – that was one of his subjects at uni – so he'd know a lot of the answers and he'd get to snort a lot in those episodes. I'd count them. 34 was the record."

"Right Would you like a biccie?" I just wanted her to blink occasionally.

"Okay." She took one.

"But the lodger's got their own telly – in their own room?" I pointed to it in an effort to drag us back to the present.

"Yes, and I never want to watch any more quiz shows as long as I live – I think I know everything I 'm ever going to want to know."

"And it must be nice being able to watch telly and take a bath without all that stress. There's the door again." And not before time, I thought.

"Hello?" another voice sounded in the hallway below.

"Come on up!" we both called, standing up and paying attention.

"I'll do the talking this time," I said. Angie didn't

object. Our newcomer was with us. I opened my mouth to say hello but this didn't prove to be necessary.

"Hello! Can I come in – the door was open so I just – nice place you've got here – lovely – You both live here – that's nice – I haven't got a problem with that – I'm very broadminded me – where can I put this? – There will do – do you do breakfast as well? Is this the window? – Nice view! – Is that the garden? – Do I get to use the garden as well? – Hope so! – Not that I'm one for sunbathing – I get a rash – but it is nice to sit out of an evening – It is quiet around here isn't it – do you mind the quiet? Gets me down a bit if it's too quiet…"

"Not really I…" Angie attempted.

"Coffee?" I tried.

But she was way ahead of either of us.

"Oh no don't do coffee – thanks – have to keep off the caffeine you know – I like to have Redbush tea that's my favourite if you've got any but don't worry if you haven't a lot of people don't like it, but I do as it's naturally caffeine free – you know – a lot of people don't realise what a powerful drug it is, caffeine, I don't go on about it like some people do but I do try to keep off it – but you go ahead with your coffee if you want to – I don't mind – I'm quite broadminded…"

"Thank you. Most kind," I think I said, but nobody heard. I nudged Angela into action.

"Um, yes," she managed. "Have you come about the room?"

"Yes," said our benefactor. "I want…"

But we were never to discover her desires as, "It's taken," I heard Angela say.

"It is?" The visitor looked at us for the first time, quizzical disbelief on her face. The same expression was probably on mine. But Angela grabbed the ball and ran with it," Yes just a minute ago, I forgot to tell you – just before you arrived, sorry you had a wasted…"

Our Benefactor looked put out. "Well you could have phoned me on my mobile to let me know, I wouldn't have come out all the way here, it was only on the off chance as I don't really like this area but I thought I'd better take a look – funny sort of area isn't it, out of the way a bit but alright if you don't want to see much life…"

"And we're just going out so…" I hinted.

"Yes, okay, well…"

"Sorry we didn't ring you, "Angela chipped in again, she was having an assertive day, I noted, "but it has only just this minute gone to someone else who was just here before you so – sorry you've had a wasted…"

"S'okay, I don't think it would've worked – it's a bit far out for me – bye."

She swept out. The silence felt soft and warm.

"Bye!" we sent after her, "you've had a narrow escape," I said. "Coffee?"

"Aren't we just going out?"

"Well, I just said that to get rid of Motor Mouth but yes, actually, I *am* going out – just called round on my way."

"Oh, anywhere nice?"

I realised she was hinting.

"Well, not really no – just meeting some of my evening class crowd – just a few of them –very few – only a lunchtime drink."

"Oh that sounds nice," she was still hinting.

"Oh it won't be," I backpedalled, "I don't really want to go."

"Ok – we could get in a bottle of wine – have something to eat here – have a chat – I'll put 'Some like It Hot' back on – we could watch that and…"

"But I really ought to go – they're expecting me – it's a sort of end of course celebration… it'd be rude not to go… just the class… you know …"

"It's only half-term."

"I meant a half – term celebration – students and

tutors. Mandarin for Beginners." I was improvising now.

"Can you all speak Mandarin now?"

"Only half of it. But enough to order a round, what more do we need?" She seemed to have lost interest – but then…

"Perhaps I could come along – try out my new singleton wings?"

"Oh – there's somebody at the door!" And there was.

"Come on up!" we called – and she did. Third time lucky, I thought, already grateful to the new visitor for interrupting at a moot point and giving me time to think.

"Hi, I called yesterday?" said our third visitor, "I'm a post-grad student at the Uni – just need somewhere for weekdays…"

But Angela interrupted her, "Oh no – sorry the room's gone!"

"Who to?" I asked. That should have been 'to whom' but I was caught unprepared. Our visitor looked from one to the other of us.

"She called a sec ago," Angela went on, "and said she wants the room – Persephone. Persephone Smith. Sorry."

Our visitor shrugged, said, "Oh, okay, oh well. I'll

keep looking, I'll see my way out. Bye." and was gone.

"Angie?" I was taken aback, "What was the matter with her? She seemed perfect? Who the hell's Persephone Smith?"

"Only name I could think of. I was in school with a Persephone Smith."

"Oh good – but why put her off – she seemed perfect?"

"Yes – exactly. Didn't she just. Perfect." She sounded bitter.

"So?"

"So – I'm not having her here in case Martin calls round. She was exactly Martin's type."

"Angie," I had to explain, "I think Allan is Martin's type right now – at least for the foreseeable future…"

But Angela was still on theme, "And she's obviously single and looking for a man – well she's not having my Martin!"

"Well neither are you," I felt I had to point out, "sorry – to split hairs, just thought I'd…"

"Beth," she said, "I don't need a lodger like that. I'm not taking the risk – I'm not winning him back from his boyfriend to have him going off with a girlfriend who… whom I've invited to stay under my own roof – a viper in the nest. She was obviously looking for a man."

"I don't think she'd be looking for Martin, she was in her twenties! Martin is an old man to her."

But she wasn't having any of that. "They go for older men that sort!"

"She could have been a nice friend to share the house with… keep company? Tell her 'Penelope Smith' couldn't make it."

She shook her head. A stubborn streak I'd not suspected.

"There's one more coming today – she'll be fine. And I can downsize if she isn't.! And it's not for long – this is just to tide me over until…"

"Martin gets back," I finished for her.

"But you don't know how long he'll be gone. And he might never…." But again I couldn't get as far as the unmentionable possibility because Angie interrupted once more.

"Just for this fling he's having – wild oats that's all. Midlife crisis. I'll show him. I'm going to be wild free and independent. Until he comes back. I don't need a lodger. Or a tenant."

"Angie, yes you do. You don't want to be poor. We don't *do* poor. You'll need a bit of extra to have nights out with me!"

"Well I'll wait and see – someone else might turn

up. Somebody just right."

"Pity you didn't say that 20 years ago!"

Unfortunately, I'd said this out loud.

"He *is* just right – he just doesn't know it at the moment."

I let it go. We got back to the painting. Discarding the pink and the yellow we cleaned our brushes and both tried the blue. Having absentmindedly dipped my brush into my coffee I paused to wipe it on the dustsheet.

"I know what the problem is," I said. "I sussed it a while ago – the problem with lodgers – relationships – marriages – the whole bit."

"What is it then?" Angela looked up from her painted oblong of blue.

"Well it's always with other people isn't? That's the problem. Always their moods and their personalities – always the same. Not enough. With a crowd you're okay – it all just blurs, loads going on so you don't notice details – but with *one* other person it's like Chinese water torture – the same thing over and over."

"Suppose so." She didn't sound convinced.

I elaborated, "I mean, when twenty people are snoring it's like white noise, you get so you can't hear it – like when you stay in a hostel it's just the background sound – people snoring – you get deaf to it – but with one person snoring it's deafening – you can't help listening to it – Or one person leaving towels on the floor – that's annoying – but when everyone is doing it it's just normal and you can do it too – towels just kept in a big heap – but with just two people – one drops the towel and the other has to be the one to pick up. I don't think we're *meant* to live together in twos – two is too intense. Clue is in the name – too two, too too much. Much too much."

"You think we should live in threes then?"

"No – in tribes. Well we did didn't we? They didn't have divorce courts – tons of paperwork every time somebody wants to split up, ranks of lawyers and solicitors lining up for their piece of the action – they just wandered off and slept somewhere else or moved to a different part of the wood and the whole tribe took care of the kids." Anthropology 101 had been interesting too.

"Hmm. It's a thought. I just can't cope with weird people being in my house. This is our house – where Hugo, our son, comes to visit. When the exchange rate allows. And I'd like it to be nice for when Martin gets back."

"Right. What happened to the wanting to get out there and have some wild times?" I reminded her.

"Well," Angie hesitated, "not *very* wild – Just a few dates – then Martin would take notice and see I'm attractive to men."

"Yeh – but trouble is – so's he."

Harsh, I know, but someone had to say it.

But her resolve was not shaken.

"Well, men are supposed to like what's not available – and what's mysterious – I read that somewhere. Probably what he saw in me in the first place. It was at a fancy dress do – I was Cleopatra, Queen of the Nile in a gold dress – slit right up the side!"

She looked misty-eyed again.

"Hmmm! That *is* a tricky image to keep up in suburbia. Right. He liked you as Cleopatra – But he left you as you are, so – change who you are! If he knows you are attractive to other men – he'll look again to see what he's missing. Is that the plan?"

She left off painting, a glob of blue fell off her brush and joined its yellow and pink cousins on the black carpet.

"How can I show him I'm attractive to other men?" she asked.

"Well," I said, "attract a few – be out and about on a few dates. This isn't the biggest town in the world – there's only one centre – word gets around – he's bound to bump into us – you – out on the town with our – your – dates – me just as chaperone of course." I clarified hurriedly.

"But how do I get dates? I don't know anybody – nobody single anyway."

"Easy," I knew this one, "do what everyone else is doing – put out an ad locally – computer dates."

She didn't like that, "Oh I'd feel silly. People would laugh. Everyone at work would know. 'Oh she must be desperate' they'd say."

"You don't have to use your real name."

"Don't you? Are you sure?"

"Yup!"

"How do you know?"

"I read it somewhere," I said, vaguely.

"Okay then!"

"Nothing heavy – just a nice night or two out on the town!" I said, persuasively.

"Scary!"

"Oh, don't worry. I'd be there. Just to get you out and about. Was it long ago you went dating?"

"A bit. If my best friend had a date we used to go to the pictures on a Saturday night with one of his friends to make a foursome. I'd always go with 'the friend'. Me and him'd watch the film and eat a lot of chocolate while the other two snogged themselves into a coma."

"Oh – *that* long ago! When did you meet Martin at

the fancy dress do?"

"At 'uni – Freshers' week. He spilled his drink on me."

"How romantic. What did you say?"

"I said sorry."

"*You* said sorry?"

"Yes!"

"And then what?"

"He accepted my apology graciously. And then vomited on my shoes."

"Ah!"

"He was very drunk. Seemed so helpless. I just wanted to look after him... He had these big sad eyes. All sort of helpless and cuddly."

"It had to be marriage did it – You couldn't just get a puppy?"

"Oh no! That was what I always wanted."

"A puppy?"

"No, marriage!"

"Oh -not wild then? Just married?"

"And I still want to be – I just want some peace and quiet when I get home!"

"You'll get there! "I said, "if that is what you want. We'll just go a bit wild in the meantime!"

"Yes," she agreed, "but I don't need 'expensive – wild.' 'Wild on the cheap' will do me fine."

"Not sure it'll do me." I was hoping for nightclubs and restaurants – not a bottle of hooch in the telly room," Speaking of which – Oops! Is that the time? Better go. It'd be nice if you could come but it'd take a while to get all that paint out of your hair."

"Okay, think we've done enough for today," she vaguely indicated the few oblong and square patches and splats on the still black walls, "and I want to watch the film again anyway, *Some Like it Hot*."

I pondered," Did they ever do a sequel to that?"

She looked blank. "No, why?"

"Oh you know, called 'But Most Prefer It Lukewarm'."

"I don't think people would want to watch that," she frowned.

I let it go.

"And," she continued, brightening, "another possible tenant's coming round later – she might be okay you never know."

I left her to it. "I'll sort out getting you out and about soon don't worry." I promised, "I'll do us a computer ad or two."

"Okay – thanks see you soon," she looked pleased. "We'll have a coffee! Do something wild!"

"Of course we will!"

I headed out as she settled down into her chair and reached for the remote.

Chapter Three

After a busy and fulfilling couple of weeks, persuading people to buy houses they didn't really want with money they didn't really have, I called on Angela again one late Saturday afternoon.

During the interim I had, of course, not been idle on her behalf: I had checked with her, of course, that this was indeed the route she wished to take then I'd put in an advert on the computer dating site – for both of us, of course – she could not possibly be alone out there. I couldn't quite see myself in the role of mere guardian, secreted in the shadows of some pub or restaurant in case of emergency or terminal boredom, so I had advertised for a double date. One must always be prepared to make such sacrifices in the name of friendship.

We had received more than a few replies and I'd

printed them off. I expected she would be excited to see them. I had, of course, to save her all that trouble, already picked out the best of them and arranged a double date for that evening. All was set for a night of adventure!

The door was open when I arrived.

"Hi, Angela – s'only me. Where are you?"

"Hi, Beth – I'm in here. Just watching the last of this…"

She was in her favourite chair watching a film. I was beginning to become unsurprised at this.

"What is it?"

"My absolute favourite – *'Cabaret'*! Amazing!"

"Another favourite? There are so many! Mind you," I brandished my paper – sheaf of promised excitement, "It's appropriate! Look what I have here," and I broke into song, "Life is a cabaret, oh chum!, Come to the cabaret!"

Angie didn't look up but turned up the sound a little – surreptitiously. I gave up and sat down.

"Yes – very nice," she said," but I do think Lisa Minnelli has the edge."

"I'll practice."

"And find a backing orchestra. Like a biccie?" she offered the plateful on a small table and I took one,

"Great film, *Cabaret*," she told me.

"Yes – I have seen it," I said, looking around. Who hasn't, I thought.

I was used to a small sherry about now.

"It makes you think doesn't it?" she said.

"Yeh – I hate films that do that," I replied, vaguely.

But there was no refreshment in evidence.

"OK. I'll put it on pause. Coffee?"

Finally!

I nodded assent.

"Got anything stronger?" I hinted.

"Ok! I'll do the cafetiere stuff."

"Oh goodie," I muttered, through a smile. "How's it going with the new lodger – sorry tenant?"

The fourth applicant *had* turned up and *had* been 'alright' – and *had* moved in the next day. Contracts signed, deposit paid. On the phone Angie had seemed resigned to having a little less space and a lot more money.

Angie shook her head, "Hardly see her – she does shift work – goes to tutorials – writes on her thesis – gets films from the library and stays in her room. She's had overnight guests sometimes though – male."

"Guests? She's only been here a fortnight!"

"Yes. I think she must get them from the library too. She doesn't go anywhere else."

"Well there's an idea. Maybe… What's he like?" I enquired.

"He? You mean 'they'? Whenever I come home there's another heart-broken male moping in the driveway asking her to let him in. Calling up to her window."

"Ah! Romeo and Juliet in suburbia? That's a sequel no-one's ever written."

Angie shook her head.

"It's not that romantic. She just tells them to 'sod off, it's all over', shuts the window closes the curtains and switches her iPlayer back on."

I took another biccie, "Juliet would never have done that."

"No," Angie agreed, "they didn't have iPlayers then."

"Do they persist – these suburban Romeos?"

"A bit. I keep a check on them through the living room curtains. Eventually they give up and wander off. I feel guilty. I want to ask them in for a coffee but I wouldn't want that to be misconstrued."

"No," I conceded, "nobody ever wants to be misconstrued these days. Not even construed. So how many boyfriends has she got?"

We'd wandered back into the living-room.

"She insists they're not boyfriends – she says she just likes 'flings' occasionally – she's very honest with them – it's only for one night – she doesn't lie to them. She doesn't want anything 'getting in the way'."

"Getting in the way of what?"

"Writing her thesis – for her PhD."

"Oh, I see, What's the thesis?"

"Romance in Modern Literature."

"Hmm. Sounds like the safest place for it. She liked the room anyway. Which did she go for in the end – the yellow, the blue or the pink?"

"None of the above – she likes it black. I agreed to paint over what we'd done but she just went over it with a marker pen."

"Oh well. That was all worth doing then. She doesn't get under your feet?"

"No… She has a system – spends a couple of days working on the thesis then goes out and fetches home another man."

I was intrigued. "How does she manage that?"

"She's got a laptop in her room."

"No, I mean how does she get all the men?"

Angela could be obtuse at times I'd noticed.

She shrugged. "Dunno. I think she just smiles at them. They all seem very nice – those I've seen. Though a bit sad. And tired. I feel sorry for her – she's obviously not able to make a commitment. I pity her."

"Pity, Angela? Is that what you feel?"

"Well yes," she replied.

"Not jealous? Nothing like a little bit of envy hidden in there?"

"Well no, of course not – she might be having a lovely time all carefree and hanging out with good looking guys and no responsibilities and studying something she loves and no worries or stress – but, Beth, does it make her *happy*? *I* don't think it does. I'm sure she'd *much* rather be watching a good film and chatting with a good friend than flouncing about out there – reading 'literature' and having loads of affairs. Out there. Playing the field. Never did anything for me. Or you. Did it? Beth?"

"Er… Well, anyway," I stammered (I have to admit I'd drifted off a little into this vision of a life of bliss)," Anyway – today's the day for *you* to get 'back out there' How are you feeling? Be good to be getting out there again?"

The film had gone into pause and Angela roused herself to take an interest in life. She looked apprehensive rather than excited.

"Out of the habit a bit," she said. "Not used to going out on the town."

"You and Martin never really did set the world alight did you?"

"Burnt the toast occasionally."

"Is that a euphemism?"

"No. We burnt the toast occasionally. At breakfast time. Set the alarm off. And we'd go and watch a bonfire in November. Had a cocoa. Never liked fireworks though."

After a few weeks away, I felt myself wading back into what felt like treacle.

"You must have got out there — into the razzle-dazzle — *sometimes?*" I tried.

"We went to dance classes when we were young," she offered.

"That sounds good, did you learn anything?"

"Yeh — don't go to dance classes. Martin liked them though. Used to flirt with everybody. Absolutely everybody. I can see why now, looking back."

She drained her coffee and poured another one. I raised the painful issue of Martin's new love.

"Have you seen them again lately? Love's young… well… Love's middle aged — dream?"

"Him and Allan? Martin and Allan? Sounds like a

double act. Only the usual – seen them hanging out in the canteen at work at lunchtime – talking – laughing – eating food."

"No sign of them breaking up yet then?"

She pulled a face. "I expect it's all for show – in public they seem to be all lovey-dovey but I bet once they get home they've got nothing to say to each other."

"It could go on for years then… that's how it works for most of us," I speculated.

"It will *not.*" She was quite emphatic. "He'll be back. It was exciting for them while it was a secret affair all hidden liaisons and stolen moments…"

"Well three years is quite a *long* moment…" I chipped in.

"… but now we all know about it they'll soon get bored. It's just a fling!" finished Angie.

"Quite a long fling," I pointed out helpfully, "Almost a whole throw… but yes, I'm sure it's just a fling like you say," as she was glaring at me in an unfriendly sort of way. "A three-year going -on four-year 'fling'. One of those real, heave-ho 'flings' – which might just put your back out."

She was looking peeved.

"Anyway," I said, chirpily, "are you ready to get back out there?"

"Not sure if I am now it comes to it."

"Oh, you'll soon be back in the swing!" I said, confidently and perhaps a bit heartily – like the PE teacher at half-time trying to hoist confidence into a team which is 8–0 down.

I recalled my own hated PE teacher with a pang of sympathy and new insight.

"I can't get *back* in. Never was *in*. Not in 'the swing' anyway," she sighed.

"Not 'swing' then," I said. "Poor choice of words. How about 'lurch'? Ready to get back in the lurch? Are you ready for that?" I was grabbing at straws here.

"Even when I was 'out there,'" she said mournfully, "I spent all my time just trying to get 'in here'… into being married and settled, to stop having to be 'out there'. I didn't really like 'out there' – even when I was."

"But 'In here' isn't all it's cracked up to be either though is it – domestic bliss?" I ventured," We get 'in here' then we just want to get 'out there' again... Well, some do," I added, seeing the offended look on her face.

"Martin *did* get back 'out there' but left me 'in here'."

"And now you're fed up with being in here so you need to get 'out there'."

"No… just to get Martin back 'in here."

"Because it works so well?"

"It'll work better – we'll go out more."

"Out there?"

"Yes, well, we won't want to be stuck in here again will we?"

"Right. Have you thought of having a revolving door fitted?" I suggested, inspired.

"No, why?"

"Oh, just a thought. You're doing well so far – You've sorted out your finances – lodger pays the mortgage…"

"Tenant. Well, actually, there's news about that."

"Oh yes?"

"Letter arrived this morning. From Martin."

"Oh yes? On his way back? So soon?"

"No – here it is – he's arranged to pay the mortgage – says he should as he is the one who left."

That was unexpected.

"Decent of him!" I consented, "– and you didn't even have to ask! Frank wouldn't like that – too much decency would put him right out of business! Decency is every solicitor's nightmare! Well… that's good. For you."

"No it isn't – I don't want him paying the mortgage – I want him back here." She was quite petulant.

"Well, it means you'll have more money for nights out… and the car and…"

"I don't *want* his money."

"Well alright – you could give it to someone who does? Or to a good cause…?"

She looked scandalised.

"Don't be ridiculous, not giving my money to some scrounger!"

"Well," I had to agree with her and backpedalled somewhat, "I know – put it away – use the rent from your lodger…"

"Tenant," she corrected me.

"… to pay the mortgage then save up for a big holiday when you and Martin are back together?" I suggested.

"*Big* holiday? Are you saying he's going to be away for *ages?*"

I backpedalled some more.

"No, of course not – a big night out then – or a little night out – tiny – a really small night out."

"That's better!" she said, in an accepting sort of voice which was a relief as I didn't have any more room to backpedal into.

"…So…" I got us back to the question of the moment, "do you want to have a look at these replies to the advert we got… Martin is off with Allan having a fling, now you just need a bit of spice in your own life."

"Just until he gets back!"

"Of course until he gets back. You can't mope around here."

"Why not? I like moping."

"But all the world is out there – waiting!" I insisted.

"I know – that's why I want to stay in here. The world is waiting. Like a leopard."

"No! Like a… fairground – a funfair – an adventure!"

"I went to a fairground once. I was sick."

"O come *on*." (I made a determined effort to shake a globule of treacle off my foot).

"You're just out of the habit of having fun. You're in the habit of being fed up!"

"I'm not fed up…!" she declared.

"Of course you are! Totally fed up – c'mon we're going out. Both of us. To cheer you up out there. You know what you need?"

"A quiet night in."

"No! You've had enough of those for one lifetime.

Just a few good times and positive experiences to get your confidence back!"

"Back?"

"OK – to *get* you some confidence. You have to go out and get what you want – not what you've been *told* you want. Something for the real *you*! You have to go out and *grab* life – and make it *happen*. I read that somewhere."

"I *did* grab at life. It *bit* me!"

"Probably in self-defence," I muttered, "But what you want has changed now. You're older, wiser – more self-aware – it comes with age."

"Well it's a lousy compensation. Look at everything else that comes with it."

"You're at the perfect age – old enough to learn from your mistakes – to know who you really are."

"I *know* who I really am. Isn't that the problem?"

"You're a different person now from when you were younger. What did you want when you met Martin?"

"Martin."

"Ok, scrap that question. But who were you *before* you met him? *That's* who you need to get back in touch with. The real you!"

"OK. I was lonely. And desperate… and scared of

dying alone so I wanted to be married."

"Ok. Ok – good – lonely, desperate and scared – so, lonely, so, what did you do about it? You made life *happen* didn't you? You did it then, you can do it now. What did you do?"

"Martin."

I could see a theme developing.

"Look, forget Martin. This is life with*out* Martin. We all make mistakes."

"He wasn't a mistake – he'll be back – you'll see- this is just a phase thing. I'm ready to forgive him. All relationships have their glitches."

"Angela, Martin's been having an affair for *three years*."

"Yes exactly – *only* three years – is that long enough to qualify as a glitch?"

"I think it is. Plus the affair is with a bloke which kind of puts an extra spin on it."

"I don't see why. Just another middle – aged experiment. All marriages have glitches. Some are just bigger than others. Mind you, yours doesn't. You and Frank seem fine though. How do…?"

"This isn't about *me*, "I interrupted her quickly, "It's about *you*. Let me worry about me and Frank. C'mon – let's get these dates organised!"

"You were very quick getting that computer – dating organised – didn't know you were good with all that technology," she looked impressed.

"Oh… amazing what you can pick up when you're, um, when you want to – not tricky at all."

"I haven't been on a date for years."

"It's like riding a bike – you never forget how."

"Don't think I ever *knew* how. Or how to ride a bike," said Angela, mournfully, "I used to go on dates sometimes – never worked though – I never got anywhere. Even when I *did* fancy them. Not so much as a snog!"

"Really?"

"Yeh, really! I did everything it said in all the magazines: I used to dress up; I used to pretend to be interested in what they were saying, I used to say nice things about their mothers; I would ask about their jobs. Blah blah: I listened quietly never mind how bored I got; I gave them compliments; Asked them in for 'coffee'. Nothing!"

"Nothing?"

"Yes! At first I thought they were just being gentlemanly – but the ones who fancied me I didn't fancy and the one I fancied just didn't fancy me."

"Gosh, and that hardly *ever* happens!"

"They could look good from some angles but

when we got close up... eugh!"

She pulled a face and shuddered. I thought that was a bit hypocritical as she'd never make a front cover herself.

"It's not all about looks though is it?" I suggested.

"Isn't it? Why isn't it? But you can tell so *much* from looks: and clothes: like whether they've got a good job or not; whether they've got a decent car or not; which designer they like. All the *important* stuff. Here's your coffee."

"Yes all the important stuff. But it's not just about that is it?"

"Isn't it though? You're going to think badly of me... I used to get, you know... lonely."

"Well – people do," I sympathised.

"I mean, you know... *physically* lonely."

"Oh, no, I wouldn't think badly of you for that. I... loads of people get *that*."

"They do? I used to sneak home and read a copy of '*The Joy of Sex*' by myself."

"Is that still in print?" I helped myself to another coffee and poured some milk.

"No, I found it in a charity shop. Most of it. Some of the pages were missing."

"Probably the best bits – nicked for reference."

"Probably. Or I'd read articles in *'Cosmo'* about 'how to please men.'"

"Got any sugar?"

"No I didn't, that's what I'm saying – I mean, you know, women have needs too – and you shouldn't go too long without it – it said so in an article. Didn't tell you how to *get* any though –though I read it cover to cover and all the small print."

"I know what you mean…" I said, then, "I mean, I think I do. As far as I remember I mean…"

I helped myself to sugar as she went on.

"You know – the *'physical* aspect' of being with someone. I used to go and try and pick someone up at the local nightclub, get them drunk, take advantage but I could never shout loud enough for them to hear what I was saying."

"Tricky, yes. Depending on what you were trying to say," I agreed.

She carried on, "And when I tried to pull them towards the door they always looked nervous and pulled away. I was on my own for years before Martin."

"It is difficult," I sympathised.

"But," she went on, confidentially, "I found *one* way to get some physical contact: I used to push in at the queues at sales so someone would push me back.

I used to go along – not to buy anything – but just so I could get squashed in the crush. It was quite exciting. All those bodies pushing me about!"

"Did you find that helped?"

"Oh yes. Once somebody even trod on my foot and I think I had an orgasm," she said, mournfully.

"I must give it a try. Do you miss Martin much… that way?"

"Always did."

"You were together for *years*, there must've been something between you?"

"An awkward silence mostly. But then we got a telly. Television was so much better in those days. All you get now is a million channels of adverts with occasional glimpses of garbage. No wonder relationships don't last any more – how can they? Me and Martin would get home from work but we did different things all day – I fill in forms and he analyses people. Not much to talk about really."

I asked, "What does Allan do – remind me?"

"He's the Company's Chief Accountant."

"Oh – so Martin didn't make off with some hunky plumber then?"

"Hell no!" She was horrified at the idea, "He's gone *gay*, Beth, he hasn't gone *common*!"

"Thank heaven for small mercies." I said. "He might still be redeemable. So you don't miss the companionship then? You're *meant* to miss that – I read that somewhere."

"I missed the companionship when I was with him, come to think of it," said Angela, "We never had much in common really. After the first few months of passion."

"You used to chat."

"True we did. We did chat. Or he did. But I hardly ever knew what he was talking about. He didn't realise. He didn't notice as long as I grunted in the right places. Kept him happy. Come to think of it, I don't think he knew what I was talking about either. He just grunted too. Sex was about the same from what I remember."

"Okay!" I intervened, cheerfully. "So… you're in a better space now! Onwards and upwards! We'll be out there tonight, cruising the bars, tasting life, meeting these two computer-date strangers – in search of romance and excitement – launching out on the new incoming tide of life re-invigorated… leaving behind the Martins of this world… off into adventure… wild and free…!"

"Yeh," she said, "where do you think him and Allan will be tonight? I'd like Martin to see me out and about if he's out with Allan. But only if our dates are quite handsome."

"Hmm, not sure." I considered, "The waterfront is quite popular. Do you think him and Allan will be into cruising the bars?"

"Shouldn't think so! Where do you go when you're middle-aged and gay?"

"Same places where people go who are middle-aged and not gay I suppose: The garden centre and quiz nights."

"Shall we try there then?"

"Doesn't make for a hot date though does it? We're meeting these two hopefuls. Tell you what – why don't we go to a few places – one drink in each – it's a small town – then we're almost bound to see Martin or someone who knows him and who will tell him they've seen you out and about?"

"Okay. But it'll be hard to see if he's there, or not, in the dark won't it?

"We could take a torch?"

"No that might look a bit odd."

"Tell you what," I had an idea, "wear your bright red coat then, even if we don't see him, it'll maximise the chances of him, or somebody who knows you both, seeing you."

"Yes! Especially if I flap it about a lot – catch their eye," she agreed.

"Yes. Almost bound to attract attention. And you thought a torch would look weird."

"What time's the bus?" she asked, fetching her bag.

"Not long now."

"Odd to be going by bus. Hope I've done the right thing."

"Don't think of it as a bus. Think of it as our chariot into the future! Into the unknown – away from the predictable and every day, mundane and boring... and we'll both be able to drink!"

"How is Frank?"

"Oh, he's fine."

Angela frowned. "He must be very secure – you coming out with me on a date and him not worrying. That's a sure sign of a really close relationship."

"Oh it's close alright. Need to open a window."

"Not if we're going out!" She was being obtuse again. "We'll be off in a minute. But... would you ever be tempted – you know... if we meet these two and they turn out to be two gorgeous hunks who invite us back to their place and you know... want to let us have our wicked way with them, you know... all night. *Might* you be tempted?"

"No, of course not! I'm happily married!" I said, seeing the trap and sidestepping it neatly.

"Even though they might be good looking, elegant, fit, with warm twinkling eyes? Sensitive… interesting… witty …?" she insisted.

I picked up the theme, "With lovely hands, with his shirt open at the neck, soft voice – *really* good at pottery… and fatally attracted to women who look exactly like me…"

"Why? Who's that?"

I'd been too specific.

"I mean *you* – women who look like *you*. Can't help himself."

"Would you be tempted?" she persisted.

"Don't see why I would be." I followed my instincts on this one.

"Good! I'm glad you're not that sort of woman! Would *not* want to associate with that kind! Can't wait – a double date – let's have another look at those messages. How many replied to our ad again? How are we going to recognise them?"

I perused my notes.

"It says here – ones taller than the other."

"That doesn't narrow it down much does it?" she frowned," People don't usually hang out in matching pairs. Anything else?"

"It says they 're both attractive. Not to what

though – Wasps? Flies? Iron filings?"

"This one says he's deep."

"He's yours. I fell in a cesspit once – *that* was deep."

"And this one says he's got a great sense of humour."

"He's yours too. That means he'll turn up with a whoopee cushion, a false nose and tell jokes about vicars all night."

"*This* one says he's intelligent."

"He's mine – all I'll need to do is agree with him all night and he'll think *I'm* intelligent too. Shouldn't fail."

"Fail to what?"

"Pull."

"I thought you were just my chaperone. Aren't you?"

"Of course yes! That's what I meant. Help *you* to pull. How are you feeling? Excited?"

"Scared. Can't we go next week?"

"Oh come *on*! We're going to have a drink and a wander around the town centre. We're not swimming with sharks. We'll just go down the pub and say hello. It's a nice place. I've been there."

"What if they're horrible?"

"No problem – so are we… Takes off the pressure. Look – yours says he's 'sporty!'… Or is that spotty?" I peered at the word.

"Sporty? Doesn't that mean he's all sweaty and forever in T-shirts?"

"Yes – actually, he's mine too," I said.

"Do you *do* any sports?"

"I've got a running machine."

"Do you do much running?"

"I've got a running machine. Doesn't mean I *am* a running machine. I switch it on and sit and watch it. It's great!"

"Right!"

"It's a start. I'll just wing it. I'll just tell him I'm 'in training and we'll be straight into rapport. They're always in training, sporty types. He'll just spend the rest of the date telling me about his 'programme', special diet and timetable of fixtures. I won't have to speak for a good two hours. Relax… enjoy my drinks… nod occasionally and then – walk him home! Sorted!"

"Do you think they'll be alright?"

"Well they were the best out of all the replies. And we had quite a few replies which is encouraging. Usually people only get two or three."

"Only 'cos you put '*adventurous*' in our profile. God knows what they think *that* means. How many replies did we get?"

"193."

"That's a lot of folk looking for adventures. *Am* I adventurous though? It *was* an advert for me." She looked doubtful.

"Well – I'm not sure if trying out a new takeaway once a month quite qualifies but it had a nice ring to it."

"Doesn't it qualify? Am I not adventurous?"

"Well," I decided to prevaricate, "it might disappoint some with the more fevered imaginations – which is most of these going by some of their replies and what *they* thought 'adventurous' meant anyway."

"Really?"

"Well they do all talk about various adventures they'd like to try – but not one of them mentions a takeaway." This was true.

"Thanks for sorting through them for me anyway."

"This one says he's fit and solvent. That helps."

"Just means he's still able to see his toes – if not actually touch them – and inherited plenty of dosh from his dad."

"It does say he's got brown eyes and a hairy chest

though."

"Hmm, "but, sister, so has Lassie," I intoned.

"Maybe we should stay in? There's a new Indian opened I haven't tried yet? And '*Curse of the Black Pearl* is on again. My absolute favourite! Brilliant! Johnny Depp in seaboots!"

"We're going *out*. Anybody can wear big boots and be amazing."

"Does help if you're Jonny Depp though," she said wistfully, "What time have you got to be back for Frank?"

"Well, erm, I thought I could maybe stay here, if we – er, I mean, you… when we get back. Frank's not expecting me back tonight. I said we'd be late and he's got an early start tomorrow. Tournament. He hates me waking him up when I come in late. We could maybe invite them back if – we like them – do you think? I thought?"

"Oh. But we're only meeting them for a drink. Aren't we? How late are we going to be?" she looked panicky.

"Yes of course. What was I thinking? But Frank *has* got a really early start."

"Has he? How early? It's Sunday tomorrow. Does he get up at dawn?"

"No, he's a solicitor not a shepherd."

"Hmm," she speculated, "solicitors up at dawn – to wade heroically through the law – to rescue the lost, helpless and innocent and pull them out of the darkness?"

"Well he *does* have a lambing season – but it's not to rescue the helpless or lost – More to impale them firmly on a good contract – and keep them well in the dark so they can't read the small print until they're fleeced. Frank's good at that."

"Well, we all have to make a living," she said, supportively.

"Yes – or a killing. I just thought it would be nice to stay out… I mean *over. Stay over.* Here. Of course here. We could talk and have a few beers. You need support. This is a big deal for you after all – getting back into dating and meeting new people and having… adventures. Who knows? I'm your friend and I'm here to support you after all in to this new phase of our – *your* lives… life. *Your* life. This adventure – wherever it takes me. *You.* Takes you. I need to be by your side and ready for any eventuality. We should go out. You should go out. We're all ready now. We can't stand them up and watch films! We're going on a night out! We never know what might happen."

"That's what worries me. Nobody knows. But we can guess! Oh – *why* did Martin leave? I wouldn't have all this fuss and bother if he'd stayed!"

"Thanks! *What* would you be doing now?"

"Much the same probably – wondering whether to go out or not – then deciding not to. I do miss it. I wonder why he left?"

"Yes it's *such* a mystery."

"It *is* easier when you're young, though, isn't it?" she said.

"Yes… What is?"

"Well, everything."

I agreed. "No – one has a personality yet to get in the way, do they, and everything's at the beginning. No regrets. No bitterness. Acres of time to make mistakes, recover from them and carry on to the next adventure… And then suddenly you're looking *back*. And all you can see is *mistakes!* It's difficult being young but you don't know it is!" I felt nostalgic for youth.

"Well nobody gets any practice. No wonder we screw it up."

"Obsessed with acne and hairstyles and if I had the right clothes. Thinking it's all about looks. That's what we're told," I remembered. "As if that mattered."

Angela nodded. "It would be nice to meet someone nice. Someone I can *talk* to."

"Yes. What about?" I was curious.

"Oh you know."

"No. What?"

"This and that. You know… as you do. Whatever's on telly. What you've each done during the day."

"But what *have* you done during the day? What *is* on the telly?"

"Well not a lot. But it's nice to have someone to ask. I'd like to meet someone interesting, you know."

"Interesting?" I queried.

"Yes, who can speak his own mind. Thinks about things."

"What things?"

"Oh you know. The world, books, events, current affairs, hobbies. Things."

"Speaks his own mind. Like Martin?"

"No not like Martin."

"He spoke his own mind – I remember he did."

"He just never agreed with a thing I said! That's not speaking your own mind, that's just being a bloody-minded argumentative sod."

"So… you want to meet someone interesting, who has their own opinions… and agrees with you?"

"Yes. Doesn't everybody? Maybe I should join a discussion group?"

"What for?"

"You know – to discuss things."

"What things? What would you like to discuss?"

"I don't know. Interesting things."

"What things do you find interesting?"

"Well… films. I like talking about ones I've seen and ones I'd like to see. Ones I liked and ones I didn't like. Things like that."

"Quite a specialist discussion group then?" I was sceptical.

"What did you put in our advert again?"

"Two friendly, adventurous females would like to meet nice guys for adventures."

"No wonder we got so many replies!"

I agreed, "All of them rather dwelt on the word 'adventurous'. Hardly any of them seemed like nice guys. C'mon, we've got a date for tonight. That's a start. That's taken a lot to organise. I… you… we… have needs. Plenty of time for discussion groups. I think you have to be alcoholic before you can join a decent one anyway."

"It's very good of you to chaperone me. But what if yours fancies you? What if I fancy yours and mine fancies you? Will you tell them you're married? Should I tell them that I am? What if we don't fancy either of them? What if we both fancy one of them? What if they don't fancy us? What if they do? What if we both fancy both of them? What if they both fancy both of us?"

"Could be a wild night."

"I know!" Angela said suddenly. "We'd better work out a code!"

"Huh?"

"To signal each other. To work out who fancies who."

"You mean whom. Yes, that's an idea. But do you know semaphore?"

"No. I know, if you fancy one of them, you rub your eye," she said, inspired.

"Which one?" I asked.

"I don't know yet – we haven't met them."

"Which *eye* I mean. Oh I know – we each rub the eye which is nearest the one we fancy!"

"Yes!" she said, grasping the principle. "We'd have to keep looking to see if we rub our eyes – in case we miss it."

"I could go first," I offered.

"Yes, but then if I missed it you'd have to rub it again. I'd have to watch you."

"Might seem a bit unfriendly," I considered.

"Yes," she conceded, "you *are* supposed to look at

people and talk to them! But I'd have to keep looking at you to see if you're rubbing your eye or not."

"I could nudge you?" I suggested.

"Yes, that'd be good. Then I wouldn't miss it. But what if they see you nudge me?"

"I'd be very discreet."

"What if I was standing too far away for you to nudge me discreetly?"

"I could always throw something at you." That idea had come to me quite quickly, "You'd better be standing very close to me so I can nudge you."

"But, Beth, what if I have to go to the loo?"

"Well, I could bring you down in a rugby tackle to get your attention before I rub myself in the eye but then they might smell a rat, don't you think?"

"Tell you what," she said, "scratch your head as a signal to get my attention so I look at you – *then* rub your eye. Left eye if you fancy him. Right if you don't."

"Ok."

"And I'll do the same."

"At the same time?" I queried, spotting a flaw.

"No – you're right – that might look silly. We'd better practice. What's first?"

"Nudge. No, Scratch head. Nudge. Then rub eye."

"Okay."

"There."

"Sorry I missed it."

"You weren't looking!"

"I wasn't ready."

"Okay I'll try it again."

"Ok… go!"

"Well *that's* no good – you're already looking! I'm supposed to scratch my head to get your attention. You look away, I scratch head until you look at me – *then* I rub my eye."

"The one nearest the one you fancy?" she said, seeking clarification.

"Yes!"

"What if they're both disgusting? Will you rub both your eyes?"

"If I don't fancy either of them I won't rub an eye."

"But how will I *know* that – I might think you've rubbed an eye and I've missed it?"

"Okay, okay!" I had a re-think. "I know – if I don't fancy either of them I'll scratch my head and then touch my nose. Nose for no – see? If I fancy both of them I'll rub both my eyes. Okay?"

"What if you're holding a drink?"

"I could always tip it on the floor." I was improvising now. The treacle was rising higher but I could see the shore so wasn't giving up now.

"Or you could hand it to me," she suggested, throwing me a lifeline.

"Or that. Yes. That'd work better," I agreed.

"But then what if I fancy one of them and want to touch an eye or a nose?"

"I'm beginning to wonder if this is worth it," I was forced to admit.

"I know!" she was inspired again, "touch your eye *if* you fancy one of them – the one nearest – or touch your nose if you *don't* fancy either of them! I'll do the same. We'll just have to put our drinks down somewhere. Eye – yes – nose – no. Scratch head – nudge…?"

"They'll think we've got fleas. I know – if you want to stay for another drink, finish your drink and say, 'Let's have another one.' But if you want to leave and you don't fancy either of them, put down your glass half empty, don't drink it, and that'll be the signal for us to leave!"

"What if I'm thirsty?"

The waves closed over.

"I give up. Tell you what. I'll just carry on drinking and scratching and if you're still there by the time I lose consciousness I'll take it you're keen on somebody. We can sort out the details later."

"What if they don't fancy us?"

"Well if they start prodding each other in the ribs and poking each other in the eye at least we'll know what they're trying to say. Let them sort that part out we've got our own problems," I took a biccie. "Maybe being married isn't so bad after all?"

"Look," Angie went on, "all this talk about fancying, we're just going for a drink – and a chat – just to see how we all get on – get seen out and about – so no pressure – if we want to meet them again we've got their phone numbers."

"Sure."

She poured another coffee. "Actually, I doubt I'll fancy either of them. It's ages since I met someone I took a shine to."

"Well," I pointed out, "you haven't been looking. Or *have* you?" I said, teasingly.

She didn't smile. "No of course not! I made my vows and I stuck to them. I believe in the marriage vows. I don't like people who play around. Can't stand liars!"

"No, you don't," I agreed, that very subject having been the topic of discussion at a few coffee mornings and dinner parties I remembered. Not so much a discussion but more a time where we had all sat drinking our coffee or eating our pudding while Angela had held forth on this issue that was close to her heart, "You have mentioned it in the past. A woman of principles," I acknowledged – in my mind's eye recalling Martin's facial expression and silence on the subject in a new light.

"Well," she continued, "It keeps it simple that way. Complicated business looking around and meeting people and seeing if you fancy them or not and seeing if they fancy you or not. Takes ages. If you're married – they're just *there* – whatever. Makes life simple and you can get on with the important stuff."

I was confused, "So… what's the important stuff?"

"Well!" she was surprised to be asked, "like where to go on holiday or whether to go out or not or which film to watch!"

"More important than who you're with at the time?"

"Well yes!" she looked at me as if I was some kind of half-wit, "– as long as there's *someone* there doesn't really matter who it *is* – does it?"

"That's very… pragmatic!" I said, tentatively.

"Thank you!" she said.

"Makes me realise," I added, "that the entire Romantic Movement was just one enormous waste of time really. All this rot about *feelings* and the need for emotional fulfilment – just took us all off on the wrong track didn't it?"

"Yes," Angela, agreed. "Not sure what you mean but, yes."

"All we need really," I suggested, "is to keep company with people who like the same kind of take-away as we do and won't snore all the way through the movie!"

"Yes," she agreed, not picking up on the questioning tone in my voice, "I *do* love a good romantic film – and it'd nice to watch it with someone else who does. Martin liked murders and quiz shows. How did you meet Frank? Was it very romantic?"

"Yes! Bumped into him in a pub… He was with a mate of his and I went over to chat him up."

"Wow!" she was impressed. "And you met someone you wanted to spend the rest of your life with! *And* you got married!"

"Yeh – his mate wasn't interested. It was his mate I'd gone over to chat up."

"Oh. But still," details were not going to get in the way here, "you met *someone* and got married!"

"Yes," I agreed, "it was the in-thing to do at the time. Might have just had a good quiz and gone home happy."

"Oh c'mon! A successful marriage! You can't knock that! That's how all the great famous romances start! Unexpectedly meeting someone you like!"

"Is it? No it *isn't* – great famous romances all start by unexpectedly meeting someone you *really* can't stand, hating them for hundreds of pages and then finding out you love them *really* in the last few paragraphs. Exactly like marriage in real life – only in exactly reverse order: the 'can't stand bit' they save up for a surprise ending. So… all you have to do is find someone you really don't like and who doesn't like you – and take it from there."

Angie liked the idea, "Yes – I could meet someone and have a long, successful relationship – at least until Martin gets back of course!"

I pondered, "*Is* a long relationship the same as successful? What about successful one-night stands? Why aren't *they* celebrated? You know – cards in the shop – 'Well done – you *scored* last night. Congratulations!… Just 'cos something goes on forever does that mean it's any *good*? Is a marathon 'better' than a 100-yard sprint? In what way? Is a party a *better* party if you've locked all the doors and no one's allowed to leave?"

Angela frowned thoughtfully, "It creates jobs."

"What does?"

"Like fracking. Or lots of other things. Like

nuclear power. Or making weapons. They always say, 'it creates jobs'."

"Who says?"

"Whoever it is who wants to get us to do… whatever it is they want us to do."

"Long parties create jobs?"

"No! Getting married!"

"Getting married creates jobs?"

This wasn't an argument with which I was familiar.

"Well yes," she continued, "like making weapons. Or building roads. Or cutting things down. Creates *jobs*!" she said, with authority.

"What jobs? You mean for vicars?"

"Yes, them too – what would they do with their time if people didn't get married – they'd have nothing to do all day and what a waste that would be – but I mean think of all the other people who need weddings to keep in work!"

"Who?"

"Well, people who make cheeseboards fr'instance!"

"Cheeseboards?"

"Yes! Well, think about it – they only get seen at weddings, cheeseboards, don't they. No one uses 'marble effect cheeseboards with matching lids' after two weeks of marriage do they? Plastic bags full of

Edam and Extra Mature in the fridge isn't it? Same with the 'boxes of champagne glasses and matching ice-bucket'. Six weeks and it's all mugs of tea and 'tinnies from the offie'. Without weddings all the cheeseboard and champagne – glass-makers would be out of work and then where would we be? If people didn't get wed the whole economy could come crashing down. All the confetti makers and church cleaners and so on!"

She'd painted a picture of economic disaster of epic proportions.

"Yes!" She warmed to her theme," and what else could they *possibly* do with their skills? Cheeseboard making is not a portable skill is it! And what about vicars? They'd all be on the dole!"

"They could still bury people!" I pointed out. "That would still need doing."

"Yes. At least there's some satisfaction in that. Job done and dusted. Not just lining folk up for... and then there's all the marriage *guidance* counsellors – what would *they* do with their time if no one got married in the first place? And the police – most murders are inside marriages you know! And solicitors – like your Frank! How would they make a living without a good juicy divorce to get into? Everybody would be on the dole? All standing around with their hands in their pockets if it wasn't for marriage."

I had to admit she had a point.

"And then there's all the cake! Bakers would all be out of work too!"

I could see her point.

"So we've got to keep it all going! Like a Job creation scheme: Vicars get people married, people make cheeseboards and toast racks and matching champagne glasses – and solicitors and police mop up the mess afterwards. They could job share."

"Yes!"

We had certainly hit on something.

"And solicitors would be out of work without divorces – so need marriages to supply them!"

It was a thought to tear at my heart strings: Frank out of work. All that paperwork not done.

"Maybe that's why vicars bless weddings?" said Angie.

"Well somebody has to."

A thought occurred to her. "Marriages *and* sneezes get blessed. Why – what do *they* have in common?"

I speculated: "We feel better when they're over? They can both be a sign of illness? They can both lead to something fatal? Can spread diseases – Victorian wives nearly all had the clap 'cos hubby was down the local brothel every night – I read that somewhere."

"That's a happy thought," said Angie, a tad sarcastically I thought.

I was on a roll. "And why *do* only long relationships get any praise. It's like an exam. Locked in for years to see if you crack under the pressure. If you don't crack up you get an anniversary card – and more cake. What's that – compensation? Mad really. One-night stands can be *great*... Why can't they bless those? Or romantic flings. Or stolen weekends of passion. They can be pretty marvellous – I've heard. So I've read. Why not cards for those? Or vicars could leap out and bless one-night stands. Would make their life more exciting!"

"Would make a lot of people's lives more exciting. Vicars leaping out of hotel wardrobes."

"*That's* why weddings are short – like adverts aren't they – just long enough so that everything looks good Anything longer than two minutes and the domestic bliss collapses into lots of shouting and slamming doors."

I felt like I'd reached an epiphany.

"What time's the bus?" asked Angela.

"I mean, why don't they bless divorces? They make people happy too! Then return all the cheeseboards. Congrats all round for time well spent! Thank you for coming. Actually, how *about* all marriages automatically annulled – after three years – unless you both really,

really, really want to renew it – Otherwise, pats on backs, copy all the photographs – keep all the friends, look after the kids, make sure they see both parents – unless one is a piece of work – Swap the furniture and the house with some newly-weds for them to use – Get their 'cool pads' in return… And all go round again. Every one's a winner!"

"Yes," Angie agreed. "Why all the blame and the stigma?"

I spotted the flaw. "Frank makes a good living out of blame and stigma."

Angie added, "And if you start swapping homes you've just put estate agents out of business too!"

"O yes! That'd be no good then. But I don't have to be an estate agent! – I could have been a concert pianist. Or a dancer. Travel the world! An explorer! Or a tourist guide?"

"You can't play the piano." Angela said, helpfully, then, "You know… I never really *enjoyed* travelling."

"You amaze me," I said. "Didn't know you'd done any. When was that?"

"When I was young. Gap year. Some of it was okay – seeing things – but I didn't like all that moving around part."

"Travel does involve moving around yes," I conceded.

"Yes and it's a pain. Bags, tickets, waiting rooms, timetables, too hot, too cold. Oops lost again!" She shook her head at the unhappy memory.

I remembered. "I was going to go hiking in the Hindu Kush once. Had to cancel. My mum had a fall."

"Just as well," said Angie, "Once you've seen one mountain, you've seen them all, I say!" she said, authoritatively.

"That's what Frank says. But I still want to get there some time."

I'd seen posters and films of the rugged wilderness.

"Get where?"

I shrugged, "Somewhere."

"C'mon," Angela was getting her coat on. "Bus'll be here."

"Okay – here goes nothing!" I checked my keys and phone were in my bag and shouldered it.

"We're a bit early," she said, suddenly. "We could get the next one."

"No I'd like to be there early and have a drink before we meet them-okay?"

"Okay – wonder if they're nervous?"

"Wonder if they're married."

"Wonder if they'll show up?"

"If they don't we could go to a club!"

"No… If they don't, mine's a Rogan Josh and *The Black Pearl*."

"Hey – we're living!"

"Is that why it's difficult?"

"Reckon. But at least we're trying!"

"I'm not ready." She sat down again.

"C'mon! Let's live while they let us. We do only get one life you know. As far as we can tell!"

"No, maybe next week. Not tonight!"

I sat down again.

"What?"

"Sorry, Beth – no can do – I'm just not ready."

"Well what am I supposed to do – we can't just stand them up?"

"You ring them and cancel!"

"What? Oh, c'mon Angie!"

"Sorry. Maybe next week. It's not as if we know them – they won't mind really."

"But why?" I asked. Tonight had taken some organising after all.

"I'm out of the habit. It's all a bit sudden. Can't you ring them? We could watch that film – and have a takeaway and you can get back in time for Frank. I'm just not in the mood."

"We're going!" I tried the 'tough love' approach.

"It's just that I'm shy in company."

"Not shy on your own then?"

"Yes. You don't have to 'make conversation' or 'get to know other people' on your own. Some of the best conversations I've had have been with me! Until I end up in a row."

She sniffed, "That would be fine too if I didn't always lose."

I tried persuasion, "Shyness is a *fine* personality trait – it can be charming. Gives other people the chance to do all the talking."

She bridled at this, "Just because we're *shy* doesn't mean we like being *bored* to death!"

"Well somebody has to communicate!" I said.

"Why? Why can't we all just shut up and go home?"

"Well…" it was hard to come up with an answer.

"I mean what is there to say that's so blinking important?" she implored.

"Um… c'mon – you. I… you need a change of scene. Just let's play the field for a while," I managed, hoping she didn't notice the note of pleading in my voice.

"Is that what we're doing? I thought you were just

coming with me to be my chaperone?" She looked puzzled.

"Well – of course!"

"Just not tonight – I keep thinking about Martin."

I put my handbag down. "What *about* Martin?"

"I wonder – Is he missing me?"

"Missing you what?"

"Being together. Our time together."

"Well… I expect he's coping as best he can – putting on a brave face."

I had never felt a pang of sympathy for Martin as I did just then.

"I suppose I should do the same. Put on a brave face."

"Of course you should! – Grab at life – make it happen!"

"I just fancy a quiet night in!"

"Another one? You've just had about 312!"

"But it's Saturday! – I always watch telly on a Saturday!"

"Angie, what was it you wanted put in the advert – 'party animal'? Which animal did you have in mind exactly?"

"Well? Why do people have to assume that 'party

animal" always has to mean the fire-breathing, beautiful, wild ones swinging from the chandelier and blinding everyone with charisma?"

"Well of course – which party animal did you mean – the escaped gerbil nobody noticed which fell into the punchbowl and drowned?"

"We can't all be the stars in the spotlight! I see myself as making a more demure, sensitive contribution to the festivities of life. Still a party animal. Just a more sophisticated, quiet party," she intoned dramatically.

"With Leonard Cohen and Suzanne Vega on the deck and people standing around looking at corn beef sandwiches? Yes, I've been to a few of those."

"Yes – I have more *hidden* qualities – depths of character – unknown talents – shades of personality undiscovered!"

"Ah. Of course you have!" I humoured her.

"Well?"

"Well what?"

"What are they? These qualities?"

"I was hoping you could tell me." I floundered, unprepared.

"You go first!" she insisted.

"Well," I thought for a moment, "you're quiet."

"Yes."

"Shy."

"Yes."

"You like films."

"Yes."

"You're quiet."

"You've said that."

"You're attractive."

"That's not a hidden quality."

"It is sometimes – when the light's not right."

"So I'm quiet, shy, and look nice in the right light? And I like films?"

"Yes – lots of people would like those qualities."

"Who exactly? The beautiful charismatic extroverts swinging from the light fittings at parties?" she challenged me.

"Yes! They don't know what they're missing. Inside every successful wild party animal is a quiet, shy party-wallflower – fighting to get out and wanting to be loved I'm convinced of it."

"Maybe I should run classes?"

"On 'How to be shy'? How to stop making friends and influencing people? How to have a quiet boring life and be happy? They'd be queueing up. How to be completely contented with being an utter nobody. Might put a few drug companies out of business, mind... They'd probably have you assassinated.

"I'm *not* an utter nobody!"

"Of *course* not – didn't mean *you*. I meant all of us. That's the way to make a fortune – write a self-help book."

"How? What would I write?"

"Oh any old twaddle – just find a way to convince people they're doing something wrong – anything – and come up with a more difficult way of doing it and pretend it'll help. Sells like hotcakes. Won't change anything but it gives people the reassuring feeling that it's their fault."

"Who says the sporty one's mine anyway?"

"Sporty' could mean anything – forever in a T-shirt, built like a ferret, jumping around throwing things or just velcro'd to the sofa all year with cans of beer – yelling at stuff on the telly over his paunch. Both qualify as 'Sporty'. It's a code they use in personal Ads."

"How do you know? Have you done this personal ad thing before sometime?"

"Now and again."

"When? You've been married for years."

"Now and again – to help *friends* – and... people tell me things. Friends of mine – They see it as a kind of sale – it's good to look around now and then and see what's on offer. Just browsing – you don't have to buy."

"Don't they put all the shop-soiled stuff in sales?"

"Bit of dirt never hurt! Have a good rummage and you might find a bargain. You have to grab the chances life brings you. But always read the label."

"I thought you were happily married," she said suspiciously.

"I am. Friends tell me things."

"You should get some new friends! I wouldn't want to be friends with that sort – Unfaithful! I wonder what it says on *my* label? One careful owner? Drip dry only? No tumbling? Used and discarded – not for recycling?"

"No – come on-you're at the exact right time of life to be doing what you're doing."

"What *am* I doing?"

"Seeking new horizons – exploring possibilities. You can't stay in here and expect life to kick your door down. People dedicated to being nice to you don't swarm to your door with invites and pressies. You've got to make an effort."

"Why?"

"Well because – otherwise – life becomes dull."

"I like it dull"

"And you won't get Martin back."

"He'll come back – no need for me to put on a false show."

"I spent ages going through all those replies. And setting up the advert."

"I'm sorry. You're a good pal. How old are they – did they say?"

"Same as us I think – old enough to know which bits you've liked of life so far – what you haven't liked – with enough time left to do more of the bits you liked and enough skill to avoid the bits you didn't: Not too young and naïve – and not too old and tired – the middle."

"Middle aged – Sounds *old.*"

"It *doesn't* sound old – it sounds middle aged – old comes later – if you're lucky – old sounds old – Then you can sit back and reminisce – Or gloat if you've been really lucky. All the stuff you've done that you've liked. At our age you can do it all again *and* do the bits you haven't done yet –to fill in the blanks."

"Haven't much liked any of it so far."

"You liked being married."

"Yes – I did – but… sometimes when we look back – maybe…"

"Maybe what?"

"Well... Maybe it wasn't – isn't – all that great."

"Oh."

"It was easier when Hugo was still home: his friends – lots of people coming and going, boyfriends and girlfriend fights, arguing over what pizza we'd have or which video or who'd crashed the car. Then, suddenly, there was just the two of us. It's too intense."

"That's what hobbies are for I suppose – to give us a bit of space away from work – and each other."

"Well me and Martin work at the same place and we didn't have any hobbies together. I liked my telly. He liked his model making. Not really a hobby – more an obsession."

"Was that annoying too?"

"Only when he glued himself to something. Wonder if that'll annoy Allan?"

"You mustn't just dwell on Allan and Martin – you need to get out and about – see a bit of life. That's what keeps me and Frank together – we spend a lot of time apart. I know you want Martin back – I haven't quite figured out why just yet, but I'm working on it – but you mustn't *count* on it. You have to get *on* with life. Try new things."

"Yes, maybe if I'd done model making as well, me and Martin would have more in common. Would have kept him away from Sudoku – that's where he met Allan. Sudoku. That's where I went wrong. I know where his club meets but if I went there he might think I was chasing him, do you think he would?"

"Are you the blindest bit interested in Sudoku… or model making?"

"No."

"Well don't do that then."

"Wonder if he and Allan will do model making? I know, maybe I could develop an interesting hobby that's a bit like model making but not actually model making – and then we'd have more in common?"

"Like what?"

"Well, making something else – not models."

"Jumpers?" I suggested, grabbing at a passing straw.

"Yes jumpers."

"Knitting?"

"Yes."

"You *hate* knitting."

"I was hasty. I could give it another try."

"Look, you need to do something you *want* to do – you need to find out who *you* are – the *real* you."

"I know who I really am. I'm really me."

"That can't be true!" I cried, "You've been stifled

– trapped in a dead end marriage – unable to spread your wings and discover all your *amazing* talents – you've spent too many years picking up towels and counting the rings in baths and bringing up a child and you've become a cipher of your former self – time to throw off this chrysalis and spread your colours in the sun!"

"Do you really think so?"

"Yes, I read that somewhere – what about all those dreams you had when you were young – travelling the world – seeing strange places – meeting fascinating strangers and exciting people, doing exciting things?"

"Oh I think that was just a whim. I think you see more on the telly don't you – you get right in with close ups – saw the Great Barrier Reef last night – amazing!"

"But don't you want to swim there yourself? See the coral, the fish, the deep blue wilderness?"

"What? Not with all those sharks about! And jelly fish – they *sting* you know."

"And what about romance – remember what you told me – when you went to Greece with a friend and island – hopped and got off with those gorgeous hunks and danced until dawn at the beach disco, drinking and laughing?"

"O god yes! I was so ill! But I don't mind a late

night now and again."

"Don't you want more from life?"

"Not really."

"I mean – I'm a happily married woman, of course – but I'm quite happy to come out with you to explore your new life and help you get started on new adventures. You know – to help you."

"Lovely, yes. I'd like to go into town – let Martin see me out and about –make him think – just not tonight. Not meeting two strangers."

"Of course. This isn't about me – it's about you. But don't you want to walk on the wild side – travel the road less travelled? Don't you ever want to do something terribly wicked?"

"Don't think so. Don't think I'd know how to. Mind you…" she hesitated, "I did put chocolate spread on my toast this morning."

"There you are – it's a start – the real you – breaking out!"

"I don't want to do anything *too* wild. Not just yet."

"Hm!" I was stumped.

"Oh I expect it's just missing Martin – when he gets back it'll all be alright again – I'll be happy again."

"How will you know?"

"Well, I won't have all these worries about going out or meeting people or what to wear or what's the point of it all and having nights out with…"

"With me?"

"I didn't mean that."

"You did say that."

"I'm too old to live the singles life!"

"You're too old not to! C'mon you can't just stay in on your own."

"I wouldn't be on my own – I'd be with Captain Jack Sparrow!"

"I think that way madness lies! What is it about Captain Jack Sparrow that appeals so much?"

"Oh I don't know – he's so wild – he's free – he can go anywhere he wants to – nothing to tie him down."

"So does he stay in watching old films?"

"No, of course not – don't be silly!"

"Right. Are you sure you won't come out with me tonight?"

"No – it doesn't feel right – not yet – you go and enjoy yourself – but will you be alright on your own? They might be weirdos?"

"Oh don't worry about me – I'll cancel the blind dates and ring up… an old friend I'd like to see."

"Oh – anyone I know?"

"No – just one of my, er, used to be a client, met at an evening class, a while ago.

We'll go to the quiz night probably – home early. Probably"

"Right, sounds good!"

"Yes but you don't want to miss Captain Jack do you?"

"No – well, say 'Hello' to the Big Bad World for me."

"Well, the small, slightly naughty world we've got around here."

"Can't get up to much at the Quiz Night!"

"No indeed!"

"G'nite then! I'm going to put my feet up. See you in the week. We'll have a coffee."

"Sure! Bye!" I said.

I stepped outside and got busy with my phone.

It was going to be a good night after all.

Chapter Four

The weeks flew by: Angela had quit phoning me at what had seemed like every other day in her lunch break to give me updates on her emotional well-being or what Martin and Allan were having for lunch or where they were sitting. I found I was able to cope without that information quite well and with fortitude. She had taken, at my suggestion, to going for walks in her lunch break with a colleague and patronising a trendy, local noodle-stand for her lunch instead of hovering behind the foliage or ice-cream ads in the canteen to spy on her errant husband. The change in routine seemed to be doing her good and the rent money was coming in handy after all.

However, it was time to move on, I had decided, so I drove around to Angela's, as arranged, having waved Frank goodbye on his afternoon's efforts at the golf-course – to be followed by his evening's consolation at the clubhouse.

"Hi! Angela! 'S only me! Sorry I'm late."

We were on so much more familiar terms by now that I dispensed with waiting at the door and just breezed in, heading to the kitchen – having long given up waiting for the necessaries to be provided. At least the kettle was still hot and I now knew where the biscuits were kept.

"Hi – I'm in here! Just watching this," came the familiar call.

Unsurprised, I arrived at the door to her living room with a mugful of the necessary, having also dispensed with the cup and saucer formality, such was the new level of our bourgeoning chumship, and a biccie. I recognised the scene on the screen almost immediately.

"Hi. Oh, that again?" I said.

"It's the director's cut!" Angela said, enthusiastically.

"Oh, good! That's where you get to see all the boring bits isn't it? Can't wait!"

"Coffee?" she offered.

I raised my mugful to show I was already replete.

"Biccie?" she offered, "I need a refill – no, I'll get it – Well… *life* has its boring bits – and you don't get to cut *them* out!"

"Just as well – wouldn't be a lot left," I muttered.

"I'll just put it on pause."

"Yes, we all have to do that from time to time."

"But that's the whole point isn't it?" she called, on the way to the kitchen, "Happy endings, no boring bits. Isn't that why we watch films?" she asked.

"I don't," I called after her.

"Can't hear you!" she called, mid-coffeeing.

I sipped my coffee and looked at the blue figure suspended in mid-air on the screen, tail awry, "No matter," I said to the empty room, "It was probably one of the boring bits. On the editor's floor. Along with most of my life. Cut to the action I say. Are you *still* not taking sugar?"

"Yes – just one. Cheers! I'll watch the rest later. Have you seen it?"

"Yes – but only once mind you, I haven't memorised it yet," I said, wasting sarcasm on an unheeding world.

"It's my absolute *favourite*! Hugo's as well. They find a new planet and everybody's blue and half naked and they all care about each other and…"

"Life isn't about caring about each other," I interrupted as she came into the room

"… Oh you look very glamorous," she said on reentry. "Going somewhere?"

She'd noticed my outfit which was a bit Saturday night I admit – but then it *was* almost Saturday night.

"Oh, not really. Just felt like dressing up a bit," I said vaguely.

"I haven't felt like that for a while," she said wistfully. "Are you and Frank going out somewhere later then?"

"No," I said, as it was the truth, "how's things going with your lodger?"

"Tenant. Fine – although it *is* just temporary of course."

"Of course! Is she upsetting your routine much? Invading your space? Leaving any bath rings?"

She shrugged, "Hardly know she's here. Think she spends an awful lot of time watching television or films."

"Really? Funny how some people do that isn't it?" I exclaimed.

"I think she overdoes it," said Angie.

I watched her face but there was not a trace of irony or self-mockery there at all.

"You do? Must be bad! Anyway, your income's sorted – rent *and* Martin paying the mortgage – life's fast lane beckons!"

She slumped back into her sofa with her coffee.

"I'll drink to that – just until Martin gets back!" she enthused.

"Of course! Wonder how him and Allan are getting on? It must be past the honeymoon stage by now... maybe...?"

"They're not married – this is..."

"Just a fling – an experiment... of course – I forgot. But even flings have a timescale – they must be over the first stage by now – the hot passion; the flush of excitement at the loved one's voice..."

"The glances across the office ..."

"...The sex all over the place... the secret messages..."

"The little presents and... er... " she was faltering already.

"The hidden letters," I continued, fluently, "... the stolen nights..."

"Oh yes, those too."

I hadn't finished yet, "... The secret phone calls; the secret meeting places..."

"Yes, those *too* – hadn't thought of *those,* "she said, a bit huffily I thought.

"... The feeling you are having a break from your mundane life – the excitement..." I went on, warming to the theme nicely.

"I think we already mentioned excitement," she said, biting her biccie a little too energetically, I thought.

"… The knowing 'it can't carry on' – but letting it carry on anyway…"

"Hadn't thought of that either – but yes I expect so…" she muttered.

"…The looking out for new outfits and new underwear…"

"I *think* the list's long enough now!" she said, a little pointedly I thought.

"… And the… What? Oh yes, of course." I quit, noticing the look on her face.

"I suppose all relationships start off that way," she surmised, "… *then* the slow decline…"

"… The gradual realisation that you really can't stand the way they…"

"… Eat…"

"… Walk…"

"Finish your sentences for you?"

"Leave toothpaste all over the sink, never wipe their feet, use too much hair wax…"

"… Hog the remote… I think Martin and Allan might have reached that stage by now – they've been living together a few weeks now – that's all I'm saying."

"Frank's *always* been bald hasn't he?" Angela said, frowning, "even when you met?"

"Yes why?" I asked, caught off-guard.

"So *too much hair wax* wouldn't ever have been a problem with you two?"

She could be very astute at the most annoying times when she wanted to be.

"No – it isn't... wasn't... I just thought it might be with someone who isn't... bald... in our imaginary list of things which can cool the passion. Imaginary passion. Of course, imaginary! You feeling better now there's someone else in the house and the bills are getting paid? Any better?" I changed the subject discreetly.

"Does feel a bit better, yes." She seemed to be content to drop the issue of hair wax.

"Yup," I went on, " – that's how it works – when one part of your life has collapsed in a heap of flaming wreckage..."

"Beth," she was cross again for some reason, "my marriage has *not* collapsed in a heap of wreckage – flaming or otherwise!"

"Sorry, Angie – what I meant was: when one part of your life is trying an experiment, having a brief three-year relationship with somebody else, of whichever gender, and has temporarily moved out of your life – you *must* make sure all the other parts of your life are in order. One: somewhere to live – that's sorted. Now we move onto two: getting out of that dead-end thing you call a job and onto pastures new!"

"But I *like* my job!"

"Since *when*? You said you find it claustrophobic, boring, you despise everybody there and you hate your boss!"

"Yes, but *apart* from that I like it."

"Onward to pastures new!" I gestured dramatically.

"But it's my *only* link to Martin now! *I'm* in the HR department – *he's* the HR psychologist and counsellor – so we see each other at work all the time. I feel if I leave that link is broken and he's less likely to… to…"

"Come back?"

"Yes."

"But that 'link' didn't stop him *leaving* did it, so how's it going to bring him *back*?" I queried.

"But I get to see him most days – it keeps me in his mind – we still *see* each other!"

"Yes, Angie – you see him – Martin – but with his new lover, Allan – or rather – his old lover whom you've only just found out about – so not all that new really – having lunch together in the canteen, laughing and eating ice-cream and you hiding by the coffee machine. Not very helpful if you are trying to move on!"

"*Am* I trying to move on?"

"The plan was, remember, to show Martin what he is missing – this new, exciting woman he needs to be back with – not the boring man he's now living with – by getting your life on track! And a new job would do you the world of good – perk you up – bring out your true self – open up new horizons…"

"Oh not again! Not *more* new horizons!" she wailed tragically around a mouthful of chocolate digestive.

"… *And* get you back to enjoying life – not focussing on what is going badly – this will help you cope and stop *wallowing*."

"I'm not wallowing Beth!"

"Angie, I was on the phone with you for three hours on Tuesday night and nothing else got a mention – not even Brexit – so yes you *are* wallowing – you have *got* to move on. I'm here to help you do just that with my wealth of experience and energy."

"What experience? When have you ever moved on?"

"This isn't about me this is about you."

"Okay – but I'm doing alright aren't I?"

"You are doing alright. You *could* be doing better."

"That's what my teachers used to say but I never did. They were wrong."

"Teachers are idiots."

"Are they?"

"Yes. They think life is all about 'learning' and 'growing' and 'using our talents' and all that rot. Never did *me* any good! Look at me – I never did any of that and I'm doing alright – big house, easy job, wealthy hubby, plenty of money. Don't talk to me about teachers!"

"Yes – you married a rich man and inherited the rest. Well done!"

"Exactly – how can learning anything help you do *that* I ask you? I rest my case!"

"*Could* I do better?" she queried.

"Better than the job you're in now? Of course you could – onward and upward. More money – more power – longer lunch breaks – the world is your oyster!"

"But I've only ever worked in Human Resources. That's all I know."

"What did you do before?"

"Dishwashing. Didn't like it much. It was tiring! Hard work!"

"Okay – forget dishwashing – but move to a

bigger firm- get away from the rut you're in."

"*Is* it a rut?" She looked offended.

"Well it's a fairly *comfortable* rut as ruts go but still a rut – you know – rut-*ty* – all the elements of ruttiness – same old, same old, going nowhere. You need to be in a *new* adventure –*new* HR adventures – among *new* people, *new* office furniture, *new* queues for the lift, *new* coffee machines – *new* people to sack and push around – *new* files of paper – you need *adventure* – what's holding you back?"

"I don't know. Gravity?"

"Who knows, you could get a promotion. You could meet a whole office full of Martins –you'd feel like a new woman."

"Suppose so. Don't think I want to start learning a whole new job or anything like that – I'm quite good at what I do. Not sure what else I *could* do… What about *your* job – that looks pretty good – I think I could do that."

"Selling houses? Well I'm *not* very good at it really."

"Aren't you?"

"No – but it's not a problem 'cos I own the company. You don't have to impress the boss when you *are* the boss. My dad was good at selling houses – so I don't have to be… He taught me everything. And, more to the point – *left* me everything," I sipped my coffee and raised a silent toast to my old man.

"Is it quite easy then? Selling houses?"

"Well, not as easy as it looks – there's a lot to it really – you have to be keen – but not *too* keen – knowledgeable but not *too* knowledgeable – give them details – but not too *many* details – be smart – but not overwhelmingly brilliant …"

"Yeh that's *always* tricky. I struggle with that."

"Get them on your side – make them like *you* – then they'll like the house, you see, then help them to see not what's there – but what *could* be there – if there's a problem, help them *not* to see it – point out the advantages – if there's an obstacle – show them the way round it – if there's a total eyesore – point them in the other direction – if all is lost with some ghastly item – tell them it's 'an interesting feature' or tell them they 'can see the potential' – they'll be too embarrassed to admit that they can't. Be friendly – win their trust – there's a lot of psychology in what I do."

"Gosh. Never know there was so much to showing people round houses. I thought you estate agents just rocked up at the right address and did your best not to lose the keys."

"It's a common misperception – with emphasis on the common." I said, letting a little frost into my tone, "The money's good – I'll admit – I do nicely – probably *could* even manage if Frank wasn't raking in his solicitor's pennies – but I earn every bit of it believe me, by the end of a day opening doors and showing people 'the master bedroom' I'm exhausted."

"Mm. Maybe I won't try that then," she said.

I sighed, "It *is* difficult in our time of life to start again – best to take your experience with you where it won't be *wasted*. You must have *lots* of transferable skills. What do you *do* in Human Resources – remind me?"

She brightened, "Oh – you know – Send out forms – collect them back in – work out if people are having too much holiday – tell people when they are being sacked – give them a new number for the job when they start – give them another form when they finish – go to meetings when they're in trouble – help to get rid of them if they're ill – or old – or a nuisance. Report them if they are. Turn down requests. File the notes away. It's very rewarding."

"Sounds fine – plenty there that any firm could use! Have a look in the paper and the websites – there. One good thing about being single is you can go your own way – you don't have to worry about anyone else."

"*Temporarily* single."

"Yes of course."

"Until Martin *realises* about me – stops taking me

for granted."

"Exactly! He'll see you moving onward and upward – more glamour, more money – *that's* always attractive. Remind me – what does boyfriend Allan do? Something very high-flying I seem to remember?"

"He's Chief Accountant. Three floors down from me. And he's *not* his boyfriend."

"His bit on the side then. Oh… accountant? Is that all? Then what did Martin see in him I wonder?"

"Beats me," she shrugged.

"What did Allan see in Martin for that matter?" I wondered aloud, carelessly.

"Martin is a *very* high-flying psychologist *actually*," she bridled, "And he can look quite fetching when he's touched up his grey bits!"

"Yes of course – silly me. We'll just have to wait for matters to run their course. Right – have you been looking in the paper – Situations Vacant? Best thing to do – when someone has moved on – even temporarily – is move on yourself. Must be positive. Let's see."

"What would you do if Frank upped and left you for somebody else?"

"That's easy: Hire an assassin."

She gasped. "Gosh, really? You are that passionate about him?" She was impressed.

"No," I admitted, "it's just that hiring an assassin works out a lot cheaper than dragging through the divorce courts – besides – he's a solicitor – what chance would I stand?"

"You'd have him killed?"

"Yes – but only for practical reasons. It wouldn't be *personal*. How could I get by if he disappeared over the horizon with his millions? Well, his tens of thousands?"

"It's not just the money though is it, that keeps you together?"

"Isn't it? Oh! No, no – of course not! You're right. Of course it isn't! It's *years* of... love and respect and companionship and..." I dried up.

"That's right!" she exclaimed.

"*Plus* I'd need his money to pay the assassin. Anyway, we're doing *your* life today – not mine. Look here. I copied it out of a book I found."

"What's that?" She looked at the sketch of 'The Wheel of Life' which I'd copied onto a scrap of paper.

"It's a diagrammatic representation of your life," I explained.

"A wobbly circle with a splodge in the middle? Is that how you see my life? It looks like a jammy dodger that's been trod on. They're my favourite as well!"

"Not *your* life – anybody's! I haven't finished it yet. It's not wobbly. It's difficult to draw a perfect circle. Only Leonardo da Vinci could do that apparently," I recalled from 'Art 101'.

"Was his life in a wreck too?"

"Probably. That's why people become artists isn't it? Why else would he have faffed about with paint instead of doing something useful with his time?"

"Might have been fun," she said, sounding wistful.

"Maybe you should give it a try?"

"I can't paint."

"You've never tried!"

"I did! 'Could do better' – that was what the art teacher said as well."

"Did *all* your teachers write 'could do better' on your reports?"

"Yes. I think they used a rubber stamp. Except PE. She said I was 'Quite Good'."

"Quite Good! Marvellous!"

"No – not 'Marvellous' just 'Quite Good '. I never got a 'Marvellous'."

"But you should have done you see – don't you see – we're all marvellous! Every child is marvellous. I read that somewhere. Childhood never lets us find our *true* selves – the things which could make us shine

– just 'could do better' and 'quite good' – what does that do to a child's heart? I read this article – said we should all try and do some art – get in touch with our real feelings."

"Real feelings? Not sure about that! What would I do with them if I *did* get in touch with them?"

"That's part of this circle – see – it says, 'creative outlet' is one part – these are all sections of your life – to keep the circle turning- like a wheel – you have to look after all the different areas of your life- keep them up," I drew in sections of the circle so now it looked like a tangerine that had been trod on.

"Do I have to?"

"Yes! And one area to look at is your job – a new job! Oh look – Here's one ad – it says, 'Creative, adventurous person required to join our forward-looking department'."

"I'm not creative. And I don't like the sound of *forward-looking*. What's that supposed to mean?"

"You mustn't think like that – of course you are – be *positive*. They don't really *want* a creative person and they're *very* unlikely to be 'forward looking' – they just put that because it sounds good – they just want someone who'll shut up, do as they're told and turn up on time. Believe me, I've never had to do anything 'creative' in my life."

"Right!"

"When they say 'creative 'it's just shorthand for 'someone who agrees with us about everything.' Trust me I know. Really creative people are just those who slob about in badly fitting clothes, making trouble and missing deadlines. Who needs them? Right, you can apply for that one."

"Doesn't it depend on what I can *do* and if it fits the job?"

"Not really – it's if your face fits. Most jobs all need the same skills these days – just in a different order – it'll be more or less the same as what you do now."

"But I've been where I am for nearly 20 years. I know everybody there."

"Yes and you hate them all."

"Yes, but I *know* them."

"We're going to scratch all that out and start again. Launch into a new adventure with enthusiasm and go-gettem!"

"Um – okay if I must."

"What do you do best in your working life? Which are the best bits you want to take with you – into your new tomorrow? What do you do *best* in HR?" I could make a good life coach, I thought, listening to myself.

She hesitated, "Um, filling in forms really… and sacking people. I like doing those bits."

191

"There you go – there's your creativity, right there."

"Where?"

"Sacking people! You have to always come up with a good reason *why* they have to be sacked – something that gets past The Human Rights Act and all that other twaddle – *sounds* humane and gets a result. Creativity!"

"O right – never thought of it like that before. Just do it really. Always have to argue with that shop steward though. Really annoying – she's always sticking up for 'people's rights' and all that rubbish. A real pain. Stops *me* doing my job!" She glared at her cup of coffee resentfully, as if the annoying shop steward was swimming there.

"And it says here," I read aloud, "must be able to cope with pressure."

"Oh I can do *that* alright – I have to put up with people crying and moaning on about 'how they're going to cope' or 'the workload is making them ill' and all that nonsense. People just have to realise that when we cut back on staff everyone has to work harder – stands to reason! Moaning on. That's a lot of pressure for me!"

"Well, there you are – shows you can cope under pressure – strength of character – copes under pressure and creative and adventurous – you'll walk in there."

"Great! Whereabouts is it? Oh – no I don't want to go *there*. Right over the other side of town! I've never been *there*. My job's okay – the pay's quite good – I don't *mind* it …"

"Forget 'quite good'. 'Quite good' is in the past. 'Quite good' is not enough to get out of life. We seek more. We have new standards," I declared.

"What about *your* job – you don't like it much," she asked.

"This is about *you* – not about me. Now then – what was your first dream?" I asked.

"I used to dream there was a monster in the central heating tank trying to get out. Then I'd wake up…" she said.

"Forget the monster in the central heating tank! I meant the dreams of your *youth* – what did you think you were going to be doing when you crossed over into the golden years of adulthood?"

"Hard to say really," she frowned.

"Try!"

"I wanted to be queen."

"Try harder!"

"Then… I wanted to run a pet shop."

"Ah hah!"

"But I don't now – animals are smelly and…"

"But what does that *tell* you about your essential soul?" I demanded.

"That I was five?"

"Yes – you were five and full of *extraordinary* hopes and dreams."

"I liked guinea pigs?"

"Of course you did."

"Their twitchy noses and they like being stroked."

"Don't we all. But what does that tell you about *you?*"

"I don't like cleaning them out, though. Disgusting little animals when it comes to the toilet department – they do it anywhere…" She shuddered.

"No!" I interrupted. "It shows that you are a caring, warm, loving person who likes looking after others."

"It does? I think it only applies to guinea-pigs though. And only as long as they're clean."

"Okay! Not much to go on but put that in the mix and see what we get."

"For what?"

"Your new job! To get you out of the rut and into something better suited to *you*. Anything else – any other dream you had – how about being an astronaut? Exploring unknown vistas of space – taking Mankind to the brink of knowledge – seeing planet Earth from the depths of Space…?"

She winced. "Clumping about in a big suit, breathing heavily with swollen feet? No thanks! Our director does that. It's not a good look believe me. I like the idea of Guinea pig stroker? Do they have those?"

"Forget guinea pigs. No don't forget them – but look at what they can *teach* you!"

She pondered. "How to nibble?"

"About *yourself*! You like to be among soft warm beings. And where *are* you?"

"Where *am* I?"

"In a *HR* department! How many soft warm beings are in there do you think?"

"Well not *that* many," she agreed, "we can't all be soft and warm – we have to get people to work. And keep them there. And get rid of them when they're no use anymore. Which is surprisingly often I'll have you know."

"Why do you have to get rid of them?"

"Oh, all sorts – they get old. Or lazy. Or they get ill – or they have an accident. Or we have to close down a section. Had to lay off 126 last month because sales had slumped. I was exhausted. It can be a really tough job sometimes filling in all those forms!

But do *I* get any sympathy?"

"Right! I think I met a few of them – they were going to buy houses but then had to pull out. Totally lost all my commission. Had to cancel one of my holidays!"

"See what I mean? No thought for others some people. No consideration of the economy! And that's what I see every day – people whingeing on about 'not enough hours' or 'too many hours' or 'not enough income' or 'not enough pension' or 'too much stress', 'too much work' – that's when I get to refer them onto Martin: He's the company psychiatrist of course so he has to show them how it's all their fault they can't cope and that it's all something to do with their home life or their childhood. He's very good at it. Got promoted last month."

"Can we quit talking about Martin?" I asked, or rather, begged. "We're talking about you – I don't see how you're gentle, caring nature can be fulfilled in a job where you have to be unkind to others."

"I'm not unkind – just reasonable. I *am* a professional after all. We have to make difficult decisions – it's not *our* fault we have to wreck people's lives."

"True," I agreed. "We can't *all* have a good wages and a decent life."

"Well of course not." she agreed, "or they'd all

think they were as important as *we* are – and then where would we be?"

"Exactly! It's nothing personal. Just business," I said.

We were in complete accord.

"Didn't they say that in a film I saw once?" she pondered. "Not personal – just business'?" She frowned, trying to remember.

"Forget films – this is reality," I said. "Anyway," I returned to the job in hand, "If you want to look after and nurture…"

"That's just with animals though," she interrupted. "Especially rodents. Small ones. Doesn't work with capybaras. Too big. They leave me cold. Or with people. They leave me cold too."

"I know what you mean. People! I much prefer houses. You know where you are with a house. You can buy it, or sell it, live in it, knock it down, buy another one, repaint it, rip out its insides…"

"Yes… and animals – they do what you tell them to do – to get a carrot or a peanut. Then you can stroke them. People just whinge and ask 'Why? Why have we got to do that? Why have we got to do this? What's it *for*?' Because I'm bloody telling you to – that's what for!" She glowered at her biscuit.

"Right. So why did you go into HR in the first

place, remind me?" I asked.

"Well, women *have* got good 'people skills' haven't we? We're kind and gentle."

"Yes – but – just that you don't like people much. Anything else you don't like about the job which might help you think about moving on?"

"Well," she considered, "you're stuck sitting down all day – most of it... Looking at a screen... in a swivel chair. A chair covered in levers and pulleys to make it fit you exactly right – but it never does. And people borrow them for meetings and if you don't get your own back you need a degree in engineering to get it to the right angle again, right height and it takes the rest of the day."

"Yes, that's really tough," I sympathized. "Anything else?"

"Yes," she was more enthusiastic now, "I read somewhere you're supposed to walk about for 20 minutes every day to be fit. Well, the canteen is only five minutes away so I have to go back and to four times a day getting snacks."

"Yeh, that's really hard," I agreed. "At least I'm out and about – showing people houses, walking about the rooms, having coffee with clients, walking round gardens, looking at them, lifting my arms pointing out the sprinkler devices. It's a good workout."

"Sounds energetic. Nice. Except the 'having coffee with clients bit', couldn't be bothered with that. Do all mine by email – saves having to talk to them. I'd like to work outdoors a bit more."

"Outdoors? I don't think *anybody* works outdoors any more do they? Nobody *I* know anyway. I just stand in the dining room and point at the garden if there is one. Not many gardens left now, they've all been sold off as building plots come to think of it. Why waste space for a garden, I say, when it can be sold?"

"There must be *some* people outdoors. Doing things, making things… for us lot indoors."

"I don't mean people who dig the drains – I mean people like *us*, real people. We all seem to work *in*doors."

"Outdoors – with animals – I *do* like animals – small ones. I could be a farmer! That's with animals." She was inspired suddenly.

"Don't you have to kill most of them though?"

"No – you get somebody else to do that bit – but sheep you don't – I could be a sheep farmer – you just take the fur off."

"Sheep farmer? But you'd need a farm – and some sheep."

"And milk – you don't kill cows, you milk them."

"You'd have to marry a farmer to get a farm.

That's what someone I know down the golf club did. Plenty of divorced farmers about. It's an option."

"Yes, I fancy that, collecting the eggs in a basket in the field, stroking the cows and cutting the hay in the sunshine, I'd have to learn to milk a cow – sitting on a stool with a bucket."

"I don't think it's quite like that anymore – it's all done by machines now with about a thousand cows – but you do get to push a lot of buttons. And from what I've seen you have to wear wellington boots, wade through manure and push cows around with a stick while everyone sits in their cars watching you."

"Wellington boots?" she shuddered. "Alright – *forget* farming- what about gardening – that's outdoors – I like gardening. I like planting flowers and watching them come up and pouring insect killer on them, and mixing up the weedkiller and spraying it everywhere – *and* you're outdoors, that's fun."

"At £7.50 an hour it would have to be a *lot* of fun. That wouldn't pay your bills!"

"How do you know it's £7.50 an hour?" she queried. "Other people manage."

"Another *sort* of people dear, not like us. We don't want to lose our standards!"

"I *do* fancy gardening though – I watch it a lot on telly. Always looks nice – lots of sunshine – build a terrace here and plant a tree there-pointing with my trowel."

"No, if you're a gardener – you do actually have to *do* the stuff not just tell others what to do."

"Oh. You sure? That doesn't seem right – I've never done *that*," she shuddered.

"Looks it too – by the look of your own patch out there." I looked out onto the wind-driven patch of long grass and dock leaves Angela and Martin had long referred to as their back garden. It had reverted to type since Angela's unsuccessful efforts to turn it into a meadow. Angela and Martin had had a falling out with their gardener the previous year and he'd never returned- some joke they'd made about his skin-colour which, amazingly, had offended him – to their utter mystification as the same gag had gone down so awfully well at the golf club that same week.

"No but I intend to sort it," she said determinedly. When the weather gets better. It looks good on the telly. They do wonders."

"Yes – with presenters and whole teams of people you can't even see doing the actual work! Real gardeners do a fifty-hour week, in overalls digging up roundabouts and weeding the verges – I think they're the only 'gardening' jobs there are these days."

"I could go freelance and do gardens for my neighbours," she surmised.

"Great – but to get by you'd have to give up eating and have lodgers in every room."

"Tenants."

"You'd have to sleep on the lawn."

"It's an option."

"Angie – I think you're stuck with HR or something like it – but the main thing is to move to a different firm. Let's have a look. What about this? Computer programmer – you work a lot with computers you could probably do that standing on your head."

"Yes," she said, thoughtfully, "that puts me in mind of my *other* dream job."

"Does it? Well there you are then – let's get an application off…"

"Yes, my dream job involves computers."

"Good – name and date of birth…" My pen hovered.

"A big pile of computers…" she went on dreamily.

"A pile?"

"A great *big* pile."

"You seem to have given this some thought."

"And a mallet."

"A mallet?"

"A *large* mallet. No, a hammer, a metal hammer."

Her jaw had gone all tight.

"Right."

"A big one. And all the time in the world…"

"And the job is…?"

"Smashing them all to *Hell*!"

"Smashing them?"

"To Hell – yes – all of them – all the computers, the laptops, the leads, the screens, the keyboards, the whole hellish mass of them, smashing them up to tiny, tiny little pieces and then breaking them up some more and possibly jumping on them. And then starting again on a fresh pile."

She had gone all starry eyed.

"Right. *Is* that a job?"

"Well it must be mustn't it? Must be *somebody*'s job? Computers conk out quickly enough and they have to go *somewhere* – must be smashed up by somebody – can't *all* be floating about in the sea killing turtles".

"That's bottles isn't it?"

"Bottles – computers – anything made of plastic."

"And metal."

"So they'd crunch so nicely as the hammer hit down."

"Are you saying you don't *like* computers?"

"You're very perceptive. I *hate* them, Beth, I *loathe* them. All that talk about animals and plants and fresh air – brought it out – I've spent my whole life sat in front of a stupid computer…"

"Computers are only as stupid as…" I started.

"You know what I'm saying! Counting things, recording things, looking up things, calculating things, printing off things – just pushing buttons on a computer as it tells me what to do next, I'm not a person I'm just the soft bit they attach to a machine!"

"Of *course* you're a real person…" I soothed.

"No I'm not! All my life – It started at school. 'Oh you like the rabbits and the guinea pigs in the pet's corner do you, Angela, why don't you look up a picture of one on your computer? Print it out, label it. Find out what they eat'. *Look it up on your computer.* Do you know which search engine to use? Find out where they come from. I didn't want to find out where they came from – I just wanted to hold one and stroke it! Why would I want to know where it *came* from?"

"No of course not! Like a biccie?"

"And then at Big School. Let's all sit here all day in front of our little screens poking about in the mysteries of the world. Let's not actually *go* anywhere or *do* anything – let's just *look it up*. Doing research – meant finding the right page and printing it off. Then…"

"I thought you liked your job…?"

"You don't need to meet people you just search their CVs and photographs and Facebook page – why bother *meeting* people when you can *look them up*? On my wedding night it was quite surprising we actually *did* anything – I was half expecting just to look it all up!"

"Right!"

"And print it out! Maybe label it."

"Not computers then," I concluded.

"Well I suppose it had better be – I don't know how to *do* anything else. In fact I don't know how to *do* anything. I only know how to *look it up*."

"C'mon, you're exaggerating."

"Switch on, press button, search – what else is there after all? *Is* there a real world out there?"

"Of course there is."

"How do *you* know – have you looked it up?"

"I've seen bits of it."

"Well I *haven't!* I haven't seen anything. I just look people up and then sack them or send them to therapy. And do they love me for it? No, they don't. Where do computers go when they die – I want to smash them up!"

"Coffee?" I suggested, a little desperately, "Maybe

not computers then? Maybe travel is the answer – get out and see the world? The real world. Interact with real people. There's loads of jobs that do that."

"Oh what's the point? Wherever you go you have to come back. And it's all the same planet. And it's all covered in crisp packets and empty water bottles or hotel complexes full of tourists trying to get away… from hotel complexes and tourists."

"Well…"

"*And* they're all looking up other places on their computer desperately trying to find the right one. And *then* you have to sit on a plane to get there – and sat next to some maniac who's stuck on a computer the entire journey looking up 50 *other* places to go. And wherever you get to its full of people who want to get to wherever it is you've just come from – 'cos they believe it *must* be better than where they are 'cos all *they've* got left is the tourist trade, hotel complexes – and oceans full of crisp packets."

"You've not mentioned any of this before. A lot of people enjoy travel."

"Yes – half the planet going to look at the other half. What if they came to look at us for a change – take pictures of *our* 'quaint local' habits?"

"You might enjoy travel."

"I thought I would. See the world they said, seek

out new cultures, explore unknown territories, unchartered waters – broadens the mind they said, new ways of life – so I went."

"You did? Where did you go?"

"Sweden."

"O yes, Sweden. How was it?"

"Swedish."

"Well, yes it would be – being Sweden – but hardly unchartered waters is it? Just like here, isn't it, only the beer's more expensive?"

"I thought I'd start out small – a careful step into the unknown. It was my first real job after uni – there weren't any here – recession they called it, you know – lots of places closing so – I went abroad. Took the initiative."

"What was it you were doing?"

"Forget what it was called. But I know I was sat in some office somewhere working with computers again – that's all I remember."

"What was it like being an immigrant? Did you do much exploring?"

She looked offended again.

"I was NOT an immigrant – I was an ex-pat, thank you very much!" she snapped.

"Oh right," I said, "sorry."

I was dying to know what the difference was between an immigrant and an ex-pat but she didn't look like she would welcome the question.

She continued, "I wanted to go skiing but I wasn't earning enough. Turned out the '60,000 a week' they mentioned at the interview translated into about a fiver a month. I nearly starved. Lived on potatoes and anchovies and had to share a flat with some idiot from Cheltenham who played the harp and had bowel problems."

"Did you meet lots of nice Swedish people though?"

"Oh, God no! Hung out with all the ex-pats. Well you never know with foreigners do you? We didn't have to anyway – there was a British pub there and everything."

"Oh that was alright then."

"Then I came back."

"Was that the worst job you ever had?"

"Not really."

"What *is* the worst job you ever had?"

"This one, thinking about it. Was only meant to be a stop gap until we got a better mortgage – while Hugo was growing up."

"Oh. And how long have you had this 'stop gap'?"

"23-years."

"That's quite a lot of gap."

"Well – it's routine – you get to feel secure – it uses my degree in business studies and…"

"Martin works there." I finished for her.

"It was nice – we could meet at lunchtime, sometimes and see a lot of each other. It was nice."

"Well it isn't nice *now*," I concluded. "He's meeting someone *else* for lunch. Well, let's look ahead – bright new future – what would be your ideal job *now*?"

"I'm stuck – I haven't got any new skills – been doing this too long."

"Well – do a course – start doing something else part time on the side and gradually slip into it once you've got the new skills? What sort of job would you like? Tell me what you'd like in a new job and I'll see what the computer comes up with."

"Looking it up – see – we even look up our own lives. Well, not computers anyway, don't like any machines really, or people, I'd like a bit of travel, I don't like sitting down too much- but not too much running around either – bit of adventure I suppose – I like a lot of money – some people – I like interacting with people – but I'm fed up with having to be *nice* to them all the time when I don't want to – teamwork maybe – nice outfits to wear – quite well paid – not too difficult or hard…."

"Right – travel money outfit – adventure – Let's see – Oh I think you'll have to be a pirate! Any good?"

"Actually. Quite fancy being a pirate. It's the boots."

"Teamwork too. You don't have to be nice to people. Some travel. You'd need a boat."

"I get seasick."

"Oh well. Scrap pirate then. How about retraining? Do an evening course – doesn't take long."

"What as though?"

"Or, let's see – here – engineering, word processing – social work – you could retrain – as a social worker – lots of people become social workers at our age."

"I want to *interact* with people not listen to them moaning on about their problems. What's in that for me?"

"Er, maybe not social work then."

"All their problems and misery – whingeing on – 'I haven't got this – this happened to me – I can't do that – I've got nowhere to live – I've got nothing to eat 'blah blah blah.' People think they're problems are so interesting!"

"Okay – er, what about teaching? There's a course here to retrain. Then you can put 'could do better' on everybody *else's* report – and get your own back?"

"Beth – teachers are *poor*. I don't *like* teachers. You have to be *enthusiastic* to be a teacher. I think anyone who's still enthusiastic after 30 must have something wrong with them."

"OK How about management? Higher management? You've been junior management a while – how about looking around to move higher up? Loads of places looking for managers. Be like a promotion. You've waited long enough for what's her name to move on. Maybe look elsewhere? You like working in Human Resources – hiring and firing – maybe just do it somewhere else. New suit. Higher heels?"

"Hm – maybe."

"Okay. Here's one – manager – HR – large concern – must have experience of management – in HR. There you go. Only a few miles away. Fresh start. Get you out of a rut."

"Oh – okay."

"Make Martin sit up and take notice – wonder where you've gone anyway."

"Yes."

"You could get that job – just apply – get an

interview. Knock 'em sideways!"

"Let's have a look."

"Another coffee? I fancy a biccie."

"What about you?"

"What about me?"

"Your *dream* job? When you were a kid? I've told you mine."

I remembered. "National Park warden. In Africa."

"Right."

"Stopping all the poachers. Saving the rhinos," I remembered.

"Right. Short step from that to selling houses then?"

"Yes well, you see things differently as you get older don't you. Rhinos will just have to save themselves won't they? If they don't want to be murdered they shouldn't have such expensive horns stuck on the front of their faces making people want to come and kill them should they?" I reasoned.

"Right."

"Survival of the fittest isn't it? And in a world that wants to buy expensive rhino horn – rhinos are not the fittest are they? I can't stand in the way of evolution. It's the market – if somebody wants to buy something then somebody else needs to sell it to them. S'only natural. People want to buy houses — people like me come along and *sell* them. Otherwise nobody would have anywhere to live would they? People want to buy rhino horn — somebody has to kill the rhino to get it. I didn't realise when I was 10 how it all works out. I *was* just a stupid kid after all."

"Oh right! Never thought of it like that."

"And everyone's a winner — someone buys a house — I get a commission — someone sells a house. Someone gets somewhere to live. Someone gets some rhino horn… poachers get some money."

"The rhino doesn't do too well out of it ".

"Well they should have thought of that before they went around growing dirty great horns all over the place."

She frowned. "A lot of people say they can't afford houses — which is weird."

"Yeh, I met one of those — a guy wanted a mortgage — didn't earn enough — well… It's survival of the fittest isn't it — people who don't earn enough will all die out, I expect, and new rhinos will evolve who don't have any horns. Then the only people left will be the ones who *can* afford houses and everything will be alright. It's not as if we *need* rhinos is it?"

"Right. That makes sense. What was his job — the guy who couldn't get a mortgage?"

"He was a bricklayer. You going to do that application then?"

"I'll think about it."

"You'll think about it?"

"I haven't given up on Martin yet you know. He could just come home and we'd all be back to normal and we'd forget all about all this turmoil. It isn't over."

"Yes," I sighed, "but he *has* been seeing Allan on the sly for years before we found out – that counts as a bit of a hint in my book that it just *might* be over!"

"No it doesn't. You don't allow for human frailty. He's slipped and fallen by the wayside that's all – just having a little fling. Alright, a big fling. I'm sure you and Frank have – well at least been tempted over the years – haven't you?"

"Fancy another coffee?"

"Okay."

"What was that?"

"Oh, just the lodger."

"Tenant. Sounds busy."

"She's just having one of her men friends round. Should be chucking him out soon he's been there since yesterday."

"Right. They had a row?"

"Not really, she just doesn't like any of them hanging around too much it gets in the way of her PhD. End of day, end of relationship usually. Seems to work for her. She might be down later. Don't think it makes her happy though."

"Right. Well. Speaking of degrees – what was it you studied, remind me?" I asked.

"Like your diploma, Business Studies. Getting rich – how to move money around and get more of it than the next guy. Marvellous. Really opened my mind."

"True."

"Much better than that stupid degree Martin did – Psychology and Geography I ask you! I mean, who wants to know about the planet or how people's minds work. I prefer Big Subjects That Really Matter. What degree was it you first did?"

"Architecture."

"Oh, of course, yes. Ready for the family business?"

"The Renaissance –The great works in stone of the Ancient Greeks – the Byzantine – and I specialised in Art Nouveau."

"Oh. Great!"

"Comes in handy when I need to explain away some lump a builder's left behind. I point it out as 'an architectural anomaly after the early Tudor style.' That usually shuts them up."

"Oh good. People can be so awkward can't they? Always asking questions and wanting to know stuff!"

"Oh here's a good one – look – HR – Deputy manager wanted – perfect for you – you would just have to move up one level – carry on but in a new place."

"I don't see why I should move!"

"To get away – stop having to see Martin every day. More money!"

"So? Why can't *he* move? He's the one who's playing away!"

"I don't think he wants to move."

"Well, neither do I."

"The plot is: you're going to move on and that will help get you and him back together – you'll once more be a woman of mystery – he'll realise he misses you – and you won't be tripping over him in the canteen every day while he's sharing his pudding with Allan."

"They don't share their pudding – it's not *that* bad. They're not teenagers!"

She looked at the job advert I'd found, "Oh, but I haven't got all *this* – have you seen the list of qualifications they're asking for?"

"Oh just make it up," I said," – nobody else has got it either, you can be sure of that – if they had all that they wouldn't be applying for a shoddy little job like that would they? You work in HR so you know that. You filled in that form yet?"

"Yes – won't take a minute – I'm an expert after all. But, Beth, I'm not going to. I don't *want* to move."

"But…"

"I'm staying where I *am*. If Martin wants to move then he can!"

"Oh!"

"How about another coffee?"

"Okay," I gave up.

There was a pause.

"I was going to ask you about Hugo," she said, pouring out the good stuff – or good enough stuff anyway.

"Your little boy in Canada? Is he coming to visit?"

"Well he might do in a few weeks and – well…"

"You are thinking Martin might not be back by then?"

There was another pause.

"Well it *is* beginning to look as if it might go that way doesn't it?" she said, with an effort.

"And you haven't told Hugo yet?"

"No."

"Ah. You don't think Martin has told him?"

"Don't think so. I had an email from Hugo this morning and he didn't mention it so... I always thought it would be *over* before I needed to tell him."

"Right!"

"So... I was going to ask you for advice about it – how to tell him you know? Maybe we could watch the film and then have a chat?"

"Okay. Yeh," I felt I could do with escape into a world of blue people with tails who haven't got jobs but, among themselves, just did what needed doing.

"We could have a glass of wine or a coffee? Or two?"

"Maybe a sherry?" I said, hopefully, "shall I get rid of these Jobs Vacant pages?"

"Yeh! There's nothing there I want. Put them in that bin."

I dumped the newspaper in the recycling bin, took the proffered amber and settled into the sofa to watch the world of kind, blue, busy people who flew – and who didn't have jobs.

Chapter Five

I had decided that I was quite enjoying helping Angela on her way to a whole new life: I had often thought that my people skills were somewhat underused in my chosen career of helping people to climb the property ladder – it was limiting: I felt I could do more in the line of opening doors and windows and showing people the way forward to whole new horizons. (As long as they weren't just more of those awkward types who just won't do as they're told.)

We had made some progress I felt, as I strolled up the driveway to Angela's house. However, the grass was still uncut and some weeds were blooming untidily among the overlong stalks. I had better have a word with her about that, I decided. What she let happen to the back garden was, of course, entirely her own business but one must not let the front garden off the leash. She couldn't go letting the neighbourhood down by becoming slipshod about the important things in life – especially now as she could afford a gardener or even push the lawnmower herself – this being the age of liberation after all. Mind you, sweating one's way around the garden wasn't *my* idea of liberation – especially if you had to do it in front of the neighbours – not if you could pay someone else to do it.

The door was open.

"Hi! Angela – 'S only me!"

"Hi Beth – you're early – I'm in here! Just watching this. Come and see – it's a classic… 'Spartacus' – my absolute *favourite!*"

"Hi … Yes, of course it is!" I watched the screen for a few moments as the familiar scenes played out, "…Yes, I see – there it is again… yeh, this is where – yup – there *that* is again, *just* like before – *and* the time before that! It never changes does it? How *do* they do that?"

"Well it *is* a film," Angela explained.

"Yup, I can tell," but the sarcasm evaporated, unnoticed.

"The slaves all organise and fight for freedom – and you get to see Kirk in a loincloth. They take on the whole Roman Empire!"

"Yeh. And then they all die. Coffee?"

"He wins freedom for his children though! "

"And gets nailed to a tree, yeh."

"His name lives forever – for everyone fighting for freedom!"

"Well, I've got mine so he can step down now, job done," I accepted a cup of coffee graciously.

"And they *could* have won if they'd marched on Rome – I read somewhere…" she said vaguely, "And him and this slave woman fall *so* much in love…"

"Yes well, life isn't about loving," I pointed out, settling down in one of the armchairs.

"Ah well," she said, "I suppose so… back to life, back to reality. We're all free now after all. I'll put it on pause." She clicked the controls and the screen froze just as a Roman legion fell under the burning, rolling tree trunks.

"Have you ever considered you might spend *too* much time watching films?" I queried.

"I've never timed myself – but I only ever watch from the beginnings to the ends." She looked put out at my suggestion.

"And just in daylight hours of course?" I added.

"Do *you* worry you spend too much time looking at reality?" she asked.

"I don't – I'm an estate agent: I don't *look* at reality – I *invent* it! So does Frank, as a solicitor, come to think of it. But we sell *real* dreams to *real* people! I conjure whole worlds out of bricks and mortar. I create new futures and imaginary lives – 'all your life will become sweet *if* you buy this house!'"

"And people buy that?" she was sceptical.

"They do if they can afford it."

"And *do* their lives become sweet?"

"Don't be ridiculous. It's a house not a chocolate factory. But they *do* have more room to be miserable in. Sorry – that should be 'more room in which to be miserable'. My bad. How's work with you?" I asked.

"Fine. Back to filling in forms – I've decided it's what I'm good at so I may as well stick with it. We should all revel in our talents – I read that somewhere."

"Did you apply for that new post?"

"Nope – I'm quite happy where I am. Well, if not exactly *happy*…"

"At least it's the misery you're used to…?" I filled in for her.

"Yeh, and if Martin wants to move somewhere else so we don't keep bumping into each other in the canteen – then he can. I'm staying put. It's *my* workplace. I must *'empower myself and take control'*. My boss told me that."

"You do that! You fill in those forms. And tell your boss you want a raise!"

"Ooh no," Angela winced, "she wouldn't like *that*."

"Yeh, let's not go mad and cause any inconvenience," I agreed.

"Yeh, I wouldn't want to intimidate her. They *are* downsizing the department after all." She looked anxious.

"Right, we must always guard against intimidating our bosses. You ready then?"

"For what?"

"For what we decided to *do* today: you tell your son and your parents all about what has happened in your life."

"That won't take long."

"*Recently* – what has happened *recently*. No more having to make up excuses why Martin isn't here," I summarised, succinctly.

"Oh *that*. I don't really have to make much up – when Hugo rings I just say his dad's in the attic fixing something or making a model and is at the tricky bit. And when I called my parents I told them he has a cold, maybe Covid symptoms, and can't leave the house for fear of infecting anyone."

"But he hasn't. By now he'd either be in hospital, better or dead. You need to put them in the picture. Open the lines of communication. I've brought the Skype. What time will it be for Hugo in Canada? This is a Big Day! Are you ready for it?"

"I never told Hugo his dad had a cold – I tell him he's doing some DIY or doing his modelling."

"For two months? What on Earth does Hugo think he's making – a rocket launcher? You need to tell him!"

"I've had a rethink-I don't think we need to do it, not like this anyway."

"What? We spent *hours* talking about this and we made lots of decisions!" I protested.

"Yeh, but we also drank lots of wine. Maybe some of the decisions weren't that good. By the time we made the final ones we *were* on the third bottle."

"Decisions always get a lot easier after the second one," I pointed out.

"Have you noticed that too?"

"Yes, years ago – when I'd wake up next to one or other of my less wise ones – Unwise – but happy days," I reminisced.

"Hmm. Anyway, after you'd gone, I decided not to wait to use your Skype – I wrote Hugo a letter," she announced.

"Oh! A *letter*? You sweet old-fashioned thing you! Will he know how to open it? Will he know what it *is*?"

"*And* I posted it. First class. Airmail. But now I'm having a rethink – I mean – does he really *need* to know?"

"Does your son really need to know what? That his mum and dad have split up? Or that his dad's run off with another man? Or you've had to take in a lodger into his old room so he can't visit anymore? Or none of the above?"

"All of the above. Does he really have to know *any* of it?"

"Which bit were you thinking of keeping to yourself?"

"Well, *all* of it, Beth, – Martin'll be back soon and so Hugo doesn't need to know – he's not due to visit for months so why upset him with unnecessary information? He's quite happy, in Canada, living his wild single life – why ruin it for him? Maybe the letter will go astray – you know the post these days."

"Angela, sit down a minute – we need to talk – about that 'Martin'll be back soon' bit: Angie, Martin has been 'seeing' Allan for three years now that we know about – he has now moved in with him – that was weeks ago – last time you saw them they were in town choosing a dishwasher together – the signs about them splitting up are *not* good," I broke it to her as gently as I could.

"Buying a dishwasher *can* be a sign of splitting up," she insisted.

"Really?"

"Yes, it shows there is no longer enough in the relationship itself and they have to bring in outside influences," she explained.

"Angela, it was a dishwasher not a couples' therapist."

"Same slippery slope!" she insisted.

"Hm, tenuous. But something to cling to," I admitted.

"Well *I* like it," she said, assertively.

"Yes, happy couples don't *need* dishwashers to fill their empty lives. It's a well-known fact," I consented.

"Well," she sighed, "I'm beginning to think I shouldn't have *written* the letter to Hugo. I should have left off telling him at least until he visits. He's a sensitive lad!"

"But that would be living a lie. You *hate* people who tell lies – you said that. You've always said that, I've heard you." As indeed, I had. Frequently.

"Well, it's not really a *lie*; just protecting my child."

"Angela, he's 32! But – just hypothetically you

know – *if* somebody didn't tell *you* stuff, if someone lied to *you* – just to *protect* you, how would *you* feel about it? *Hypothetically*?" I ventured.

"Oh *that* wouldn't happen," she declared with confidence, "I can *always* tell when people aren't being honest with *me* or when they're hiding something – I *never* lie – that's an absolute principle – but this is different. I'll only tell *one* lie –just this one – a *fib* really – then go back to *not* telling lies."

"Just a slightly bendy 'absolute principle' then?" I sought clarification.

"Only *slightly*," she insisted.

"As in 'I never tell lies until I want to' kind of principle?"

"Yes!" she was glad I understood.

"It's quite a biggie though isn't it – as fibs go?" I hinted.

"It's alright. Needs must."

"You can't just have a principle then just chuck it over board when it's inconvenient," I protested.

"Why can't I? Everyone else does!"

"Well no – that's like… that's like," I hunted down an example. "That's like not parking in disabled spaces 'on principle' – until there's nowhere else to park that's near enough – and then just helping yourself!"

"Doesn't everybody do that?"

"No!"

"Well you do!"

"Well yes *I* do – but I'm always in a rush, though, aren't I," I explained, "so that's different! *I* always have a lot to do."

She really could be pedantic at times.

"Yes of course," she agreed, with a frown. "Anyway, Hugo will have *had* my letter by now."

"He'll understand. Is he still on his own? Still single?" I asked.

"Oh yes, thank God. He has lots of flings but nobody serious yet."

"He always was lucky," I mused.

"He always listens to me… I *drummed* it into him all his life – 'You stay single… have a wild time before settling down – don't disappoint me!' It's different for boys don't you think – they *need* to sow their wild oats don't they? *And* I'm not ready to be a grandmother yet anyway – that would make me feel so *old*!" Angela said.

"Yes, expensive things, grandchildren. Especially if they live in the colonies. We send ours cheques – lots of cheques. Seems to keep them happy."

"I'd like them *eventually* of course. Grandchildren."

"Why? You didn't much like having a child from

what I remember? Speaking of parents – when are you telling yours? You can't keep on telling them 'Martin's busy'. He would have worked himself into a frazzle by now. Will they be very upset – they'll take your side won't they?"

"I don't know – they really liked Martin. 'The son they never had' and all that."

"They had your brother," I queried.

"Yes, but he wasn't the son they *wanted* either," she explained, "Maybe I should go over for a visit and tell them – over a nice meal? Sit around, as a family, and talk to each other all about it?"

"Families talking to each other? Always makes me uncomfortable. Doesn't seem natural somehow."

"Well we *do* talk but it's usually about the weather," she clarified.

"You've got it easy. My parents live in the south of France – the weather's always 'lovely' so there's not a lot to say."

"That sounds hard," she commiserated. "What does your Frank make of all this? Have you told him about my life's upheavals? Martin going astray? Was he devastated?" Angela asked.

"Well, I did tell him the highlights – but *The Golf International*'s on at the moment so he's a bit distracted. I think he tuned out a bit when I was giving the details

He asked me where you were going to keep it now – then I realised he thought 'Allan' was yours and Martin's new dog and that he'd gone astray for a day."

"He likes golf doesn't he? It's good to have a passion," she enthused.

"Yes, I think so. Does one good. Keeps you young," I agreed.

"You're so lucky, you and Frank – him with his golf and you with – all your dozens of evening classes – it seems to work well."

"Oh it does. *Very* well," I agreed.

"I sometimes think I'd be better off as a man," said Angela, "they get more freedom don't they?"

"To do what? Hang around in bars, falling over?" I was sceptical.

"Well it's a *kind* of freedom. And they can do what they like – you know, sexually. Cake?"

"Yes please. If they can find someone to do it *with* – sure. What is it you're wanting to do anyway?"

This was unchartered territory, conversationally, so I was all ears, so to speak.

"Well, you know. This and that," she said, vaguely (and disappointingly and annoyingly.)

"I've only tried this – can't recommend that. But I'm sure it could be organized," I said.

"Women aren't allowed to have *fun* are we? Even as a kid I thought it was unfair. The toys we had at Christmas. I'd have a doll or a dolls' house – or a pram -or a set of dolls' clothes – or a doll who would wet itself or a doll that would puke or one that fell over and cried …or a toy ironing board."

"Bit of a theme there," I agreed. "Almost as if you were being trained for something."

"But my brother Georgie would get a *fort* – full of toy soldiers and guns, cannons and everything. Or an aircraft carrier. And helicopters. With toy Napalm and hand grenades to chuck. With a miniature all-purpose machine gun – just to get the point across. And pretend uniforms *and* bandages – junior-size body-bags *and* artificial blood just to add to the fun. He'd have such a time playing with my dad and all the uncles. I'd be giving Tiny Toes a bath, cleaning her backside or playfully wiping up her sick – while they'd all be in the dining room, wearing camouflage paint and leaves – shooting sticks at each other and shouting 'mow the bastards down!'. Looked so much more *fun* somehow."

"Couldn't you have joined in with them?"

"Sometimes they'd let me run the '*field* hospital 'or make the tea – for all the dead and wounded, but *that* was all about bandaging limbs and wiping bottoms too. Or they'd pretend that Tiny Tots was the enemy and want to torture her – one of my uncles was ex-MI5 so he knew all about that – I quite enjoyed the throwing grenades bit but mum would get cross and say it wasn't 'ladylike'." Angela was looking angry and gripping the cake knife with what I considered to be quite unnecessary force.

"Right! Do you want to put that knife down now? That's quite enough cake for me thanks," I tried. But she was on a role and kept brandishing it.

"And *then* George would want to play with Tiny Tots but he'd get a slap and told that was for *girls* and all the uncles would laugh at him and he'd cry so they'd laugh at him some more."

"Ah the magic of a family Christmas! Here, would you like a spoon?"

I managed to prise the knife off her and replace it with a dessert spoon.

"Yes. The wonder of childhood!" she muttered darkly.

"Top up?" I suggested.

"Please."

"Here and I'll just pop this back in the drawer shall I?"

"What's all that you've brought anyway?" she looked at the box I'd carried in on arrival, "Looks heavy."

"Well, I didn't know you were going to *write* to Hugo – I knew this could be difficult, telling him what's happened, so I stopped by the library and got out a pile of those self-help books – helping people talk about difficult issues and all that."

"O great! Let's see: "She opened the parcel, "Oh. *'Breaking the Silence – Let's Talk about Divorce'*; *'What shall we tell the children?' 'When Mummy and Daddy aren't friends anymore?'* This one's in cartoons!"

"Well you are addressing his *inner* child. He's still *your* child, your little boy. Divorce is never the same when it's your own parents – no-one is ever prepared for that. You'll have to break it to him gently – this could scar him for life – these books could be a great help to him."

"Did your parents divorce?"

"No, of course not – they didn't need to – they had separate houses. Daddy got some *really* good deals – a perk of the business."

"You seem to know a lot about divorce?"

"Frank is a solicitor, remember, it's our bread and butter."

"Bread and butter?"

"Well okay – bread, butter, quite a lot of jam, cake, caviar and pheasant au foi gras," I admitted," plus five holidays abroad a year so, yeh, bread and butter doesn't really come into it. What can I say? Divorce pays well. You think these books might help Hugo?"

"Shall I read them to him over the phone?"

"Well you could."

"Or wait until he's here and in his hammock?"

"Hammock?"

"His room's still full of lodger. I thought I'd put a hammock up in the dining room."

"Cosy! And you mean 'Tenant'. Hey – they might hit it off…?"

An idea had occurred to me… Hugo and the tenant in a whirlwind romance…

"No, they might *not!*" she said, flattening that idea – which I thought was a pity.

"Okay – read them to him or he could read them himself, he *is* a big boy now," I pointed out.

"They say divorce is reckoned to be the main cause of kids growing up not being able to have relationships! I don't want to destroy his chances," she said anxiously.

"He seems to be doing okay from the news bulletins you give me. Up to his *knees* in relationships," I countered.

"He does, doesn't he! A real jet setter! My boy!" she said enthusiastically.

"Though I don't know why they pin all the blame on divorce. What about all the years where everybody's shouting and yelling, throwing things and plotting murder, *before* the divorce? Isn't that reckoned to have *something* of an effect?"

"I *wasn't* plotting murder," Angela objected.

"No, of course not. It was total wedded bliss," I had perhaps a hint of sarcasm in my voice.

"We *were* very happy. I watched my films and Martin… did whatever *he* was doing. Analysed people at work. Analysed me when he got home. We watched telly together. Went on holiday. Still don't see why he had to leave really."

"It's beyond me! Makes no sense at all. What *was* he thinking? What about these books then? What about this one?"

"*'How to Tell Your Kids About Divorce'*. Oh my god it's about 500 pages long! How can I read *that* to him? The phone bill's going to be through the roof!"

"But, Angie, will your letter have been a *total* shock to him? Have you given him *any* hints before? Has he ever suspected why his dad's not here when he calls?"

"Not really, I just say he's not here – which is true."

"And you've not been dropping any hints?"

"No, I've just been phoning him weekly, as usual, and we talk about the weather. As usual."

"How does that go?"

"Well, you know, rain here, snow there. It doesn't go far as a conversation but it gets us started."

"Then what?"

"I ask him about his work. Then he tells me about it."

"Oh right. Interesting?"

"No, but he likes talking about it. Then I ask about his relationships. And he tells me about them."

"He doesn't find that a bit nosey?"

"Oh no – we're very close! – He's always told me everything. I've always taken an interest. I've always drummed into him, 'don't you settle down too soon – you play the field – have fun – don't get involved' and he's doing just that. He tells me *all* about it. Well, not all, but you know. He tells me about who he's met and I point out what's wrong with them. He always takes my advice."

"Whom," I corrected, "The people he meets… is it… women?"

"Oh yes, very much so. Always has been. Mind you, always *was* with Martin too – until Allan hove into view," she said, bitterly.

"Maybe you should start following your own advice?"

"Hm?"

"Like you advise Hugo to do – play the field a little?"

"Beth! I wouldn't want to be *that* sort of woman! What would people think?"

"'Lucky sod' I should think," I responded, truthfully, "Well – maybe then *you'd* have something to tell Hugo for a change? Can't be easy – he's the one who has to provide all the entertainment and the gossip."

"It *isn't* gossip – he's exploring his own nature and the world of relationships and looking to me for sound advice!"

"He's done more exploring than the Geographical Society – what *is* he trying to find?"

"It's different for boys!"

"I'm not so sure."

"He's like Errol Flynn… Or Alfie… Or Rudolph Valentino…"

"Or O'Malley the Alley Cat?"

"No, he *isn't*! He's having a perfectly respectable, glamorous singles life – living life to the full – my son… a healthy sexual appetite."

"Just as well he's not a daughter."

"Well, no, of course," she pulled a face, "I'd hate

to be the mother of a slut – I'd have to disown her! But I'm *sure* Hugo is only able to enjoy his life because of the secure, safe upbringing he had in our safe, secure home and happy relationship!"

"No doubt."

"And now I've told him – in a letter – that it's all over – in pieces – gone! It'll ruin him!"

"Well relationships *do* end. This won't be the first," I suggested.

"It isn't ended! It's just on a bit of a pause. Martin's just…"

"Experimenting, yes! You said. A good, *long* experiment!" I sighed.

"I don't want Hugo to see his mother as a failure – a ruin. A woman who can't keep her man!"

"Well seeing how her man wanted a man, and not a woman, you're keeping him would seem a tall order."

"He's only *temporarily* gay."

"Of course. Just a phase," I had to agree.

Angela frowned, "Funny how it's only gay people who have 'phases' – it's never a *phase* when you're heterosexual. Why *is* that?"

"No idea – though maybe it was with Martin?"

"No *this* is definitely a *phase*. But will Hugo *hate* his father?"

"Didn't he always?"

"No – of course not! Those were just rows about ordinary teenage stuff: he wanted to play his music and his dad wanted to switch it off. So he did. That's what the on/off switch on a radio is for! Building relationships. Then he'd want to grow his hair long and his dad would make him cut it short. Then he wanted to have a *band* – I ask you! Just teenage nonsense! Drumkit and guitar he wanted! Well that's not a *career* is it? And what would the neighbours have thought! And he wanted to go out with his '*mates*' instead of extra tutoring – I mean to say! Martin wasn't having any of that, of course. He said *he* didn't go out with *his* 'mates' when he was young so why should Hugo? And quite right too. Well you can see his point can't you? Then he wanted to be an artist – you know – painting and all that nonsense – we soon put a stop to that I can tell you. Not a job for a man!"

"Yes, remind me again, why *did* he emigrate?"

"Oh, he always fancied Canada – likes the snow you see."

"Does he like being out there?"

"*Loves* it. Never wants to come back! But I know the happy childhood we gave him will stay with him forever wherever he goes."

"What does he do out there again?"

"Oh, he designs stuff for the music company he helps to run. One of his pals got it started and offered him the job – flew him over specially. He did a course or something. Thanks for these books, here you are – but I don't think we'll have a problem – Hugo and I always been able to communicate, I can say that much."

"Great. Well I expect the letter will have done the job – at least it will all be out in the open now."

"Do you tell *your* kids everything, Beth?"

"What's that music I can hear? That your lodger? Sorry, tenant," I said, ignoring the question – which was rather intrusive, I felt.

"Yes, I get her to turn it down if she leaves it on too long."

"I don't see much of her. Does she go out a lot?" I asked.

"She comes back a lot too. Usually with male company and a film to watch."

"Films? You've got a lot in common then?"

"*No*! She watches all the rubbish. Arty-tarty stuff. *Foreign* most of it. She watches them *all* the time. I'd *hate* to be like that."

"Right. Is it working out okay having a lodger... tenant?"

"Yeh fine – she does what she does, I do what I do. It's only temporary of course – until Martin comes back and we can get back to normal."

"Martin doing what he does and you doing what you do?"

"Yes. Normal. It'll be nice to get back together, be a couple again. I don't think I could do what *she* does – off with a different guy every week."

"Well it might make a nice change. You never know."

"No! I'm a decent *one- man* woman!"

"Well maybe choosing a different one man to be a one man woman *with* would be a start – seeing as how your one man you're one-man *with* also seems to be a one man *man*."

"You can say that again!"

"I really don't think I could."

"But, you know Beth, I've been reading about it, you know, people who… change course midway – you know Oscar Wilde?"

"I've heard of him – Writer? Witty? Famous? Dead?"

"Put in prison for being gay – but *he* was straight until he was in his 30s so – there you go."

"There I go where?" I didn't follow.

"Well, it's not that *unusual*. It wasn't his wife's *fault*. Just the way things *are* sometimes," she said, this time waving the spoon about but in a more relaxed way so I didn't feel threatened.

"Angie, I don't think anybody's going to be saying this is your 'fault'"

"I bet they *are*! I bet they have been saying it. I bet my parents will. I bet Hugo will. Everything's *always* my fault. Even Martin will say it's my fault – and he's a psychiatrist so he should know."

"Look, Angie, supposing I met somebody else and wanted to be with them – would that be Franks' fault. If Frank took off with somebody else –would that be mine? People change – happens all the time."

"Ooh! Don't talk like that! I feel all shoogly – you and Frank – you've always been there like… well like…" she hesitated.

"Like?" I prompted, curious.

"Like rocks."

"Rocks?"

"Well, *stability*, in my life – a beacon to the rest of us – married bliss – to show us all how it *should* be done. A firm foundation," she said.

"Great. Now I feel like a patio." I disliked the analogy.

"Where *is* Frank today?" she asked.

"Oh, off on his golf course as usual I expect – how should I know? Or watching it on telly. Or… something."

"Well if you've told Frank, and I've told Hugo – I only need to tell my parents and then everyone'll know."

"How will *they* take it? Your mum and dad?" I had met them at Golf Club functions on occasions and would not relish having to tell them anything even slightly untoward. So I never had.

"Badly I expect. They hate anything unsettling. They like everything to be *just so*, you know. How can I *tell* them?" She looked suddenly panic-stricken.

"Just tell them?" I suggested helpfully.

"But *how*? They always wanted me to be *happy*."

"When did they think you were happy?" I was amazed.

"They thought the world of Martin."

"They did?" I was amazed some more.

"Yes! They came to the wedding and everything. This will destroy them!"

"The wedding was 20 years ago – have they not seen him since?"

"Oh yes! At Christmas. Most years. They got on like a house on fire. He was like the son they never had — my brother George being such a disappointment. Martin would talk about his job and listen to them talking and say nice things. It was nice. They'd cook us dinner. We'd eat it."

"Sounds heavenly."

"How can I tell them — that all *that* is over?" she wailed.

"C'mon don't upset yourself. People move on — your parents know that. They must have had their ups and downs too?"

"I suppose so. My mum would get upset about him and his women — but he was always discreet. Most of the time."

"Oh. Good. That was alright then. As long as we're all discreet," I sipped my coffee, discreetly.

"It was like that in those days," she went on, enthusiastically, "people stuck *together*. How it *should* be. He always came home. Eventually. That's how it was. They've been together 60 plus years. Be celebrating this year. Martin'll be back by then of course."

"You haven't mentioned *any* of this to them then? Not dropped any hints that all is not well?"

"No, like I said, if they ring I just tell them he's fixing something in the loft."

"All this time? They must think the roof blew off!"

"Maybe I shouldn't tell them — just wait for this all

to blow over? They don't *believe* in divorce – anymore than I do. They don't believe in people being gay either."

"So… what… think people are just pretending?"

"Well you *know* – they follow the Bible really," she said, by way of clarification.

"Well you're dad certainly doesn't – the way he carries on," I had to comment. "Which bit does he follow exactly?" I wasn't very familiar with the tome in question but I seemed to recall some quite clear statements about affairs outside marriage and such. Especially such.

"Well, he doesn't follow it *slavishly* – he just picks out the best bits," Angela justified her dad.

"And you're mum's in a new coat every time I see her!" I observed.

"What's *that* got to do with it?"

"Well, is she *ever* going to get around to helping out 'he who has none?' – you know, sharing out her wardrobe full of coats – I seem to remember someone in the Bible mentioning…"

"No of course she isn't – that's just a saying! Nobody takes that seriously!"

"Yes. Of course, just one of *those* bits… 'Pick and choose' that's what I say. Works for me! I hear the *Readers' Digest* is doing a condensed Bible – with all the unnecessary bits taken out."

"Sounds good!" she missed the irony entirely, "I don't think my mum and dad would like to think I'm single –not that I *am*!"

"No, of course not!"

"I'm just *temporarily* single

"Of course you are – just until Martin gets back – from being temporarily gay."

"Yes," she agreed, "I mean – they *know* what single people get up to."

"What *do* they get up to – remind me?" I was all ears.

"Well… copping off with each other and stuff – for a night or two."

"Sounds inviting. Must try it sometime. Not sure anyone says *'copping-off'* nowadays though." I pointed out.

"Well, whatever they call it now – It's what *single* people do."

"Of course it is, yes. Well, *some* anyway – *you* haven't shown much interest in that department so far."

"I'm *not* single! Only *slightly* single. For a bit"

"Of *course* you are. But you could pretend for a little while and come out for a beer or two? Have a look at the scenery – even if you're not setting out to explore any of it. I'd keep you company. No trouble at all. Just say the word!"

"Not yet. I've got to tell all my family first and see what they say, help them through this crisis. I don't want to do anything which will upset them more – make it more difficult."

"Right. But – shouldn't *they* be supporting *you*?"

"Oh, they're not very good at *that*. If you tell them there's a problem they just go all… disappointed – so I… don't," she said quietly.

"Have there not been problems – before?"

"Oh yes, the kitchen tap burst; the coach on the trip round Scotland broke down; the guinea pig died, I wasn't made prefect, Hugo failed his maths, Martin got ill…"

"And your mum and dad were *disappointed*?"

"Yes – they've had a lot of disappointment in their lives."

"Why are they disappointed with your brother George, may I ask?"

"Oh, they wanted him to be a doctor but he turned out to be a *palaeontologist*. I ask you!" she spread her hands in exasperation at her errant brother's wicked ways.

"Yes. Enough to break any parent's heart!" I

exclaimed.

"I mean, they *so* wanted to show him off to their neighbours," she declared.

"And they couldn't brag about him being a palaeontologist?"

"It's more difficult to brag about something that nobody's ever heard of... and if you can't spell it," she explained.

"Is he happy? Your brother?"

"Delirious! Charging about the mountains in South America with gangs of other dinosaur freaks – why wouldn't he be?"

"And what about you? Are they disappointed in *your* job?" I asked.

"Not really – it's different for girls isn't it – they always wanted me to marry a doctor – and I *did* – well, a psychiatrist and that's the next best thing. They can't spell that either – but neither can anyone else so they were safe."

"Right! And your *own* job? Your career? What *you* wanted?"

"Well it keeps me busy," she shrugged.

"Good. All good then. This will just be a blip, a slight glitch?" I concluded.

"Oh, no – they'll be *very* disappointed – they'll

want to know what I did wrong. What made him leave…"

"Is disappointment their only response to *whatever* happens in life?"

"Yeh, I think so, same for everybody isn't it?"

"Well no, not really: Anyway, you *didn't* do anything *wrong*. Martin is gay – well he is now – not his fault, not yours. Why should they be disappointed?"

"It's just what they do. And, well, they think gay people are only gay because women aren't women enough and men aren't men enough."

"Right. So, they reckon if you were more of 'a woman' – Martin would not have left you for a *man*? They haven't quite grasped what gay *means* have they? Mind you, I don't think *my* family would like it if I got divorced. Not sure if Frank's parents would either. Then I'm not sure if they'd notice if he had someone else with him instead of me. Unless it had a beard. They might notice that. We don't speak much."

"I don't see much of Martin's folks either," Angie continued, "Except at Christmas of course They come around with the rest of the family on Boxing Day: Martin's dad gets drunk and goes to sleep and his mum gets drunk and picks fault with my cooking. The nephews and nieces bring round their toys and the uncles tread on them. Hugo rings me up from Canada and we all wish him Happy Christmas.

Suppose that will all stop now – another loss, another chapter in the unfolding tragedy. What on Earth do single people *do* at Christmas?"

"Whatever they damn well please I should think. Fancy a biccie?"

"Ooh, yes, go on then. They don't know what they're missing. I feel sorry for people on their own at Christmas."

"Yeh – smug bastards."

"Hugo always goes to a big jet-set party in one of the roof apartments in Ontario with all his friends. Usually comes home with somebody gorgeous. He's got a flat in the city centre. Still, you know you've done a good job with your kids when they…"

"Sod off. Yes. Makes it all seem worthwhile," I chewed my ginger nut meditatively.

"Did *you* enjoy being a mum, Beth?"

"Sure," I said, through a mouthful of crumbs, "Employed good nannies. What's not to enjoy?"

"Didn't you feel you were missing out?"

"Yes, *that*'s the bit I enjoyed. Not much point in marrying a rich solicitor if I have to wipe my own kids' sick off the floor. That's what prep schools are for aren't they?"

"Yes, Martin didn't believe in those. As a psychologist he was very strong on mothers being at home with their kids. That's why I was always part-time. 'A home-maker'. Hugo would be round at his friend's or at school, Martin would be at work and I'd be at home, home making."

"Ideal!"

"Yes, Martin was very keen on family's spending time together."

"Well, that's turned out well!"

"What about *your* kids – did being away at school harm them? Are you close? Do they tell you stuff? About their lives?" she asked, curiously.

"Oh yes. Not much of interest though. One grandchild did *this* at playgroup – that grandchild did *that* – they went *here* for a meal – going on holiday *there* – blah- blah – all pretty ho-hum. I think I'm supposed to gush and all that – but I'm not the gushing sort really."

"And do you tell them about *your* life? All *your* little secrets?"

"What do you mean?"

"Well you know – cosy chats on the phone – getting their advice?"

"About real estate yes – they know a lot about that."

"Do you talk to them about, you know, emotional things?"

"Like what?"

"You know, about how you really *feel*."

"How I 'really feel' about what?"

"Well anything."

"Why would I want to do *that?*"

"Like another biccie?" she offered.

"I wonder if Martin has told *his* folks yet?" I said, declining the offer, "Not easy – 'coming out' it's called isn't it? Will they throw him out do you think?"

"He doesn't live with them."

"Figuratively speaking, I meant. Will they accept this new version of their little boy?"

"Well he is 52 so he's not *that* new."

"What are they like – his folks? Up to speed with modern society and the flexibility of life?" I wondered.

"Well his dad was a psychiatrist as well – like Martin – so I shouldn't think so. Has theories about everything. Likes analysing people and telling them what's wrong with them. Martin likes doing that too."

"Sounds fun. I'd have made a good psychiatrist – anything you don't like the look of you can just say that's a 'mental illness' or an 'unconscious act'. Easy. Anything you *do* like you can say 'well that's the natural order of things, how it *should* be and can't be changed. What was it like living with Martin – him being a psychiatrist?"

Angela looked thoughtful. "Had its good points. Good income. Regular hours. He *was* interested in his work. Didn't drink. Was never violent or anything. But anything I wanted out of life was either a neurosis, a perversion, a misplaced subconscious desire, or 'an unconscious need to usurp my father' – that was his favourite – or something wrong with my hormones. I *did* have an awful lot wrong with me."

"And… you want to get back to that?"

She sipped her coffee.

"Well, it's normal. I want *normal* back. *My* normal. You'd miss Frank if he left you wouldn't you?"

"Of course I would. All the time. Once I'd noticed," I agreed.

"My folks are going to be devastated – they do get cross about anything they don't like. I could never rebel in my teenage years – they didn't allow it."

"Maybe they won't be? Devastated? A lot of people get more mellow as they get older."

"When does that start?"

"Only some people. I don't intend to. Why should I? I've only just got to know what it is I want so I'm hardly going to give up on demanding it!"

"What *is* that then?"

"What?"

"What you want?"

"Was Hugo a rebel in his teenage years?" I asked.

"No – no, he was a very serious student – once we'd got him past the 'I want to be in a band and be an artist' stage. We had to really put our foot down. He brought home a guitar – one his mates had given him. Martin dismantled it. And he wasn't allowed to see those friends again. Not the right sort at *all*. But when he'd matured past that stage, at last, he'd go up to his room very early, straight after supper, and be in there studying hard all night – even at weekends! He'd have a big sign on his door saying Do Not Disturb and he'd wear earplugs so he couldn't hear us when we called out *goodnight* to him. He'd be asleep by the time we went up. *Such* a good boy. I'd sometimes creep in and he'd be fast asleep, right under the bedclothes – right over his head they'd be – and I'd creep past and close the window without waking him."

"Why did you have to close the window?"

"Well, he always left it a bit open for fresh air he said and sometimes the rain would be getting in. There was a big tree just outside – it's still there – and a branch reached right up to the window and I didn't want it rattling on the glass and waking him up. *Such* a good boy. Never gave us any trouble. Right up until he emigrated. Pity his results weren't as good as you'd expect after all that studying. Still, he worked hard that was the main thing. He was always so tired as well. No. he didn't rebel – we were good parents. Oh there's the post!" She stopped as the letter box rattled in the hallway.

"Anything interesting?" I asked, "Among the usual piles of magazine selling us stuff we never knew we needed?"

"There's a blue envelope! With stamps on it!" she exclaimed.

"What on earth can that be?" I said in mock amazement.

"It's from Canada!" she said in real amazement.

"Well, yeh, I'd guessed that much."

"What does it mean?"

"He's written back?" I took a wild guess.

"He didn't phone!" she declared.

"That's true as well," I agreed, in the face of overwhelming evidence.

"It must mean he couldn't face talking to me. He must have got my letter. Oh why did I send it?" she groaned aloud.

"Because you didn't want to keep lying to your son?" I suggested.

"And he couldn't *stand* a phone call – talking to

me! He *hates* me. He's devastated. He could only put it in writing. He's in emotional agony. What does he think of me?" Her hand went to her forehead and stayed there.

"Well… opening it might give us a clue," I suggested.

But she kept staring at the blue envelope in her hand.

"How many times has he struggled to write this letter? How many false starts has he ripped up, screwed into a ball and flung into an overflowing wastebasket in the small hours of another tear-filled day. How long has it taken him to find the right words?" she gasped, tearfully.

"Well… you posted yours ten days ago – it's five days each way so it's got here pretty much by return of post so… didn't take him *too* long. Here, let me…" I held my hand out for the letter. Patience has never been my strong point.

"Here, *you* open it." She handed it over, "I know I've *ruined* him, I've *destroyed* his life. I'm a failed mother. The centre of his little world has been *ripped* apart. This is the *end* to our mother – son relationship – he'll probably never trust another woman…"

"Well not quite. Here – have a read. I've just read the first sentence. I'll get some more coffee," I handed her back the thin, pale blue papers.

She took them and started to read, "Oh my god! O my… O good grief… I can't bear – oh – hang on a minute… What!" She was aghast – her lips moved as she kept reading, her eyes getting wider.

"What?" I queried.

"No!" she gasped.

"No?" I echoed.

"No. I don't believe it – how could he *do* this to me? Have you *read* this?"

"Well just the first part where he said he's…"

"'Delighted!' Did you read *after* that?" she demanded.

"No."

"Listen, 'he's *delighted* I've told him – 'cos now *he* can tell me some truth too. About… about his life… that he's been keeping a secret for so long…!"

"Oh no! What *about* his life?" I guessed at his meaning immediately and thought 'poor Angela, first Martin, now Hugo,' You mean he's… Is he…as well…?… Oh Angela!" I exclaimed in sympathy.

"Yes!" she confirmed," I can't believe it. All those lies! All that *deceit*!"

"Oh, Angie this must be a total shock. You mean he's…?"

"Yes – Married!" she blurted out. "Has been for *years*!"

"Married? To…?" I was still not clear.

"Oh… to someone called Shirley!" She spat out the name.

"*And* Shirley *is*…?" Ambiguity still hung in the air.

"Someone he met his first week in Canada!"

"And Shirley *is*… ?" I pressed, needing pronouns to know which way to jump.

"Oh I don't know, he says she's a musician or something!"

"She? Right!"

One needs the limitations of pronouns at times to decide what to think. Hugo was married to someone called Shirley who identified as a woman – all was clear. I sipped my coffee and let her get on with the drama.

"Yes! He says he 'never felt he could tell me!' Met her the same week he went out there! She plays the *violin*! Shirley! She's older than him and… She's been married before. Got two kids – and they've had two *more* – I'm a grandma! To four kids! And I never knew it! I've got to sit down!"

"You are sitting down".

"Lie down then. Pass me that stool."

She put her feet up and lay back as if in a swoon. She perused the letter again.

"How did they meet?" I asked, just to keep the

conversation flowing.

She re-checked the letter quickly, "He says they met at a *protest*!" she read.

"A protest?" I had heard of such things and seen pictures on the news: My overriding impression was 'scruffy'. No one of my acquaintance had ever actually been on one of course.

"Yes," Angela went on, "a protest 'to stop Climate Catastrophe', he says here."

"That's just a big myth though isn't it?" I pointed out.

She read from the letter again, "He says all the snow is disappearing and that Global Warming is real!"

"Well, maybe it is in *Canada*," I conceded, "I'm not worried – Canada's a long way away. How do you feel?" I asked.

"Dizzy. And a bit surprised," she had her hand to her forehead. "He's enclosed pictures, they're wonderful. Lovely children. They look so happy! "

"Does he say why he didn't tell you?" I asked.

"He always wanted to," she read on, wide-eyed," – every phone call – he says here – every time he visited – but I was so full of wanting to know about his wild single life he felt he couldn't disappoint me so he just made stuff up and… it got complicated."

"Even the rooftop parties?" I asked, disappointedly.

"Especially the rooftop parties! They spend New Year at home!" Her face registered shock and outrage.

"And the wild sexual liaisons and one-night stands?" I asked, hopefully – but the disappointments kept on piling in after each other.

She read from the letter, "He says he fell in love with Shirley and has been in love ever since. 'Would never want anyone else.' How could he *do* this to me! I'm so disappointed! And he says here 'She'd take the kids to her folks or stay home when he came here. 'I was worried you wouldn't accept her. Especially with her being a bit older and with someone else's kids and…' He didn't want to upset his father – Martin was always very old fashioned about things like that."

"Well he's one to talk!" I pointed out.

"I haven't got used to this yet!" she sighed.

"Was Hugo upset about his dad? You know – about him suddenly being gay?" I wanted to know.

"He says he's 'surprised' – he says here. 'Surprised' – but said he knew me and his dad had' not been in love for years.' Said he'd always known it. Isn't that weird? He says, 'you don't choose who you fall in love with' and 'he didn't expect to fall in love with his Shirley – they were friends – musicians – he thought it might be a fling at first' – I think he told me about it at the time – but it just didn't end. They fell in love. How weird is that? So he's 'been making things up ever since – telling me all about flings and parties – while really he's been at home with his wife and kids –who'd've thunk? 'You don't choose who you fall in love with'… I suppose he's right there."

"No he isn't –" I pointed out, "that should be 'whom' not 'who'."

But she was perusing the photographs.

"And something else," she said, quietly "Shirley's not…" she paused.

"Not what?" I asked.

"She's not… well…"

"She's not well?"

"No, she's not…"

"She's not what?"

"Well… not…"

"What's she not?"

"Well, you know…"

"I don't know, no. Know what? Not what? What is she not?"

"She's not white."

"Oh!"

I paused.

"What? But I thought you said she plays the violin!" I said, perplexed.

"She does – and brilliantly according to Hugo," she said, scanning the letter once more.

I sipped my tea. "That's confusing," I said.

Angela sipped hers, as the world quietly re-arranged itself around us.

We looked at the photographs. Skin shades were various. Expressions of contented delight were striking in their similarity.

"Yes, they do look very happy," Angela said," And I thought he was living the wild life! And he says having a gay dad is 'pretty cool.' Don't suppose he'll think Allan is 'cool'. Can you be 'cool' if you're fat and bald?"

"Possibly, with a lot of effort," I considered.

Anything seemed possible suddenly.

"A secret marriage! I'll put these photos up here – have to learn their names. O my god! I need to go and tell *my* mum and dad – they're *great*-grandparents suddenly!" Angela exclaimed, getting up at last.

"Hmm," I considered, "four sudden great-grandchildren; Hugo is married, has been for years; Martin's left you, set up house with Allan – his gay lover; Hugo's wife and children have more melanin in their skin than *they* do; Allan is fat and bald: They 'll have *quite* a lot to take on board your mum and dad – maybe break it to them over two visits? Soften it as much as you can. M*aybe* keep quiet about Allan being an *accountant*. *That* could be the last straw," I suggested.

"They'll struggle with the race thing,' she said, quietly.

"Yes," I agreed. I had met Angela's parents after all down at the golf club occasionally. I had felt quite at home with them of course but... Hugo *was* Angela's son and *she* was their daughter-in-law and *they* were their great-grandchildren. Something was going to have to change.

"Yes," continued Angela, "it was always drummed into me that I mustn't mix with... people who are... not white. Who could come to my birthday parties and who couldn't. I didn't realise the reason for ages. They were always clear about that. They were always clear about everything."

"Yeh, they didn't mix much did they?"

"Well no, always avoided 'the wrong sort' – and that included black people; Irish; Jews; Moslems; Asians..."

"That's quite a list..!"

"... Italians... South American... foreigners... immigrants... Travellers... Welsh... Chinese... Dad really didn't like Scots much either," she paused for breath.

"Didn't they ever get lonely?"

"Yes. Add to that anyone they thought might be gay, divorced or bankrupt and there was hardly anyone they could speak to. They were a bit suspicious of anyone with diabetes too. And with my mum being allergic to cats and dogs that about put paid to everyone else."

"I remember your dad banging on about how' immigrants were ruining the country' – when he wasn't banging on about how the Earth is really flat, the moon landing was all done on a beach and women shouldn't be allowed to drive," I recalled our few encounters over the years.

"Yes, he *did* have a wide range of bangings-ons," she agreed, "He used to do them in rotation. Nice to have a variety. Not heard them lately though," she frowned, "All's been a bit quiet on the bangings-on front. Don't know why."

"And didn't your mum do all the driving?"

"Yes," she nodded, "not much choice after he'd had his licence taken off him."

"Right – but do you think you *should* tell them – about… you know… do you think you should avoid…" I hinted.

"No! I'm going to tell them here and *now*!" she had

suddenly come over all decisive, "I always remember Rahab – my best pal for weeks at school!" she was suddenly angry, *"She* couldn't come to my party – I was only 6! I didn't *understand* – We couldn't be friends after that… Give me that Skype! Please!"

"Have they got Skype?"

"Yes, they use it for telling George in Patagonia how disappointed they are. Give me a minute." Signal's better in there – good… yes, they're in. Mind if I shut the door – this could be tricky? Here, read the rest of his letter if you like. See you in a minute." She disappeared into the next room with the device for communication.

I went into the kitchen.

Well, I mused, as I put the kettle on, it *is* a funny old world. So many surprises! Secrets jumping out from behind every piece of furniture. But it never seems the right time to tell mine. I suppose one more wouldn't hurt. No, Angela's got a plateful already. And I never liked sharing the limelight. Might all be over soon anyway. I took my coffee into the lounge and sat on the sofa. But that's what Angela says about Martin though, isn't it? '*Will all be over soon.* 'Doesn't look like it. Not with dishwashers in the offing. Must watch that. How soon is 'soon'? Will it all be over by Christmas? Who can tell? Hope her folks take it well. Wonder how mine would react? They'd be okay. As long as there's enough sherry and coffee one can cope with most things, I'd noticed. Not that that would ever happen of course. I sipped my coffee and nibbled a biccie and watched a bit of the film. Then I heard a door opening.

Angela reappeared.

"You won't believe *this*!" she said.

"Oh don't tell me," I took a wild guess. "Your mum and dad have been divorced for years but never told you; your mum's joined a lesbian commune, your dad's a Hell's Angel and on weekdays they live on the moon?"

"What? No. Don't be silly! Have they?" She looked panicky.

"No – I was just… things seemed to be going that way. How did they take it all? How did you tell them?"

"Well…" she gathered her thoughts," they started on about the weather as usual but I just blurted it all out. I was going to break it to them gently but it just all burst out. 'Martin's left me and is living with another man, Hugo's been married these past six years and you've got four great-grandchildren with dark skin'."

Well it was succinct anyway I had to admit.

"Golly! How did they react? Did they faint or scream?"

"Not exactly. My mum said, 'That's nice dear, don't worry there's plenty more fish in the sea' and 'when can they all come to tea?' and 'did I know Georgie's gone and bought a snowmobile and what a waste of money that is?' What *is* it with my family and snow? Dad's all focussed on a possible 'skin cancer' he's got, I could tell he's scared – hasn't told me about it before – and mum trying to get her second hip replacement. Not much interested in my private life or who Martin is or isn't in love with after all. Really pleased about the grandkids though. Showed them the photo of Hugo with Shirley and the kids and they went all gushy. It was odd. They don't usually do 'gushy'. Didn't say a thing about what colour they happen to be. Dad got all teary saying whatever happens to him he knows life will go on now he's seen these 'beautiful children'!"

"People *do* have such strange priorities don't they? I didn't know your dad's got a cancer scare?" I said.

"Oh it's probably just another wart," she said impatiently," wanting lifts to and from the hospital at all hours, I ask you, people are *so* self-centred aren't they? They think the world revolves around them. Fancy a biccie?"

"Aye go on! Let's live while we can!"

"Well that's that then. They're told. Bit of an anti-climax really. I was expecting Hugo to have a fit about Martin and my parents to go into raptures of disappointment about Hugo. People are so unpredictable aren't they?"

"They didn't even kick off about Allan?"

"Not a word. They've changed somehow," she said, thoughtfully, "They said 'all this campaigning for the right to gay marriage and rainbows everywhere' – made them think. Dad said his physiotherapist is gay. And black. Nice guy apparently. Got him walking again after his fall. And my mum's surgeon is from Syria. Sorted her other hip right out. No pain at all now."

"*I* never had a problem with it – the right to gay marriage," I said, not altogether honestly.

"Nor me," said Angela, embellishing in a similar way.

"I mean why shouldn't they have the right to be as miserable as the rest of us I *ask* you? Thanks," I took a biccie.

"And Hugo – it was a bigger shock – all the stuff he told me – this life I knew nothing about! Amazing. My little boy – a daddy! And I'm a grandma! I feel older already. Not as bad as I thought. Oh *look*, 'Brief Encounter' Is coming on!"

"Oh goody!" I said sarcastically, as the credits rolled up on the screen.

Chapter Six

Autumn was setting in by the next time I called on Angela. The damps of Summer were drawing to a close, giving way to the pre-washes of Autumn which would precede the onset of the heavy duty spin wash that Winter had become – when children in nurseries would gaze at the snowy scenes on the greeting-cards they had made, stuck with cotton wool and glitter, not so much in wonder as in total bafflement. But for now the crisp, blue sky days in the riotous colours of Autumn, which I seemed to remember, had just softened to a blurred, reliable, monochromatic grey.

As I pulled into Angela's driveway, I noticed the lawn had been cut, the hedges trimmed, the car washed and the borders manicured. It looked like Angela had taken my advice and hired the services on offer in the locality – either that or the neighbours had cracked under the strain and waded in to do what was necessary to save the tone of the neighbourhood and civilisation itself.

I sat in the car for a while to ponder the way forward.

Should I tell her? Maybe I should have told her before now? End of the friendship maybe, such as it was? Drive away, not tell her and let the friendship fade? She was expecting me though – I'd checked with her that I could come around this afternoon.

The door was ajar.

"Angie? S'me!"

"Hi Beth! In here!" She called from the living room, "I'm on the sofa – just getting to the best bit!"

I had a momentary vision of her on the sofa with some handsome gardener, 'just getting to the best bit', but the vision slipped away discreetly as I opened the living room door to find her ensconced, as usual, with coffee and flickering screen. The sofa was present and correct but, disappointingly, was not the harbour of any goings on which could be described as at all indelicate.

"Hi," I said, breezily. "How's…?"

"Hold on!" She had raised a hand like a copper on point – duty back in the times of our ancestors, before traffic lights, "Have you ever seen *Groundhog Day*?"

"Seen it? I seem to be living it."

"My *total* favourite! Don't want to miss this bit!"

"From what I recall, if you did miss any bit it would be on again moments later, you just have to wait…"

"Do you know the plot? He has all this time and he uses it to do all these *amazing* things!"

"Right. Does he watch many old films?" I enquired, inquisitively.

"No, of course not! Why would he do that?" she frowned, her eyes never leaving the screen.

"I have no idea," I confessed.

"Oh… *there* it is… *love* that part – really sad – But in the end he's really living!"

"Yes, well life isn't about living is it?" I pointed out, sitting down.

"Here, I'll put it on pause. You alright, Beth, you look a bit peaky? I'll put the kettle on. Coffee?"

I decided to 'take the plunge' – as they say (whoever 'they' are who keep saying pertinent things, off-stage, at various junctures of our lives.)

"Tea please," I said.

She raised an eyebrow at this, but I confirmed with a nod. Best to prepare her for a surprising visit, I thought.

"Well, have a seat Angela," I invited her, incongruously, as it was *her* house after all, "I need to tell you… Well, when you've got the drinks… um…"

But she left to go to the room with the kettle. I stayed on the couch, looking at Bill Murray – frozen in space as the truck lurched over the cliff. I too felt like I had begun something I could not stop.

"Um, Angie," I began again, calling after her. "… Hate to tell you this – but… er, something's *happened*… and… I thought you should be the first to know."

She came back in with the necessaries on a tray.

I tried again, mumbling and gushing in turns. My voice sounded strange to me in both mumbling and gushing modes, I noticed.

"Why? What's happened?" she asked, "You look very serious. Sugar?"

"No, thanks," I said, "it's a low-carb day. Yes to milk though. It's Frank."

"Frank? Frank's happened?"

"Yes."

"Oh, my god! Is he… is he in hospital? It's all those cigars and all that golf!" She had frozen halfway to her own cup with the spoonful of the wicked white stuff.

"No – he's not in hospital – he's quite well – It's what he's *done*."

"Oh – good! Oh no! What? But why are you looking so… *What*'s he done?" She stared at me.

"He's left me," I heard myself say quietly.

"What! I thought you were going to say he's won the golf tournament!"

"No, he came second. Again."

"Oh!"

There was a pause.

"Would you like a biccie?" she said, handing me the packet.

"Please. Thanks."

"There you go… But *why*?"

"Well it's nearly 11o'clock and I *am* a creature of habit," I explained.

"No! Not 'why the biscuit?' Why… that other thing!"

"Because the club secretary always beats him?" I said.

"No, not 'why did he come second' either – the bit before that – Why… left you?"

"'Why *did* he *leave* you?'" I corrected her.

"You, not me," she corrected me.

"It's all come out!" I exclaimed, leaving grammar to lie where it had fallen.

"Don't worry I've got another one," she said, taking the biscuit packet from me but seeing, in surprise, that the biscuits *hadn't* all come out.

"Not the biscuits, I mean the *truth* – the *truth* has all come out," I said.

"Oh! *That!* Well… it does that sometimes. But it's probably just all a mistake. It usually is. All a *'misunderstanding'*, when the truth comes out. Usually. Would you like a Garibaldi?" she offered.

"No… sorry… you don't *understand*," I said.

"Oh don't worry I *do*! I only keep them for emergencies – the bits get stuck in your teeth don't they? How about some bourbons?"

"No, not biscuits. There was a message on the answer machine," I said.

"There was? I can never get mine to work. How…?"

"I don't know how! He found it somehow. He must have known which button to press."

"Frank? I thought you said he never…?"

"On the *phone*, Angela, the button on the blessed *phone*! There was a message and a button on the *phone*!"

"Oh that's nothing I'm always getting messages I can't hear properly, or left for the wrong number – some guy was breaking his heart last week *begging* someone to ring him back. Obviously a wrong number – he *thought* he was talking to the love of his life. Desperate. I was going to phone back and let him know he'd rung a wrong number but I'd just sat down and…"

"This wasn't *like* that," I interrupted, "it was a *very* clear message and it was for *me*!"

"Frank left you a message on the ansaphone?" Angie dunked her biscuit and glanced up at me for confirmation.

"No! Frank *heard* a message on the ansaphone!"

"A message that was for you?"

"Yes!" I began to glimpse dry land up ahead.

"I bet it was offering to mend your broken computer?"

"No. We don't *have* a broken computer."

"No, we haven't either – but it doesn't seem to bother them though does it – they just keep ringing back and offering to fix it."

"This wasn't *about* computers!"

"I sometimes feel guilty – that I ought to go and break it just to make it worth their while – all those phone calls and I always disappoint them!"

"It wasn't about broken computers."

"What then? That lot always trying to sell double

glazing?" she said, sucking the coffee out of the biscuit. It occurred to me how less formal our coffee meetings had become.

"Not double-glazing, no."

"No, it's still a bit early for them," she dunked the biscuit again," bit later in the year they start – I bet it was the ones wanting to sell you life insurance – they *never* give up – leaving messages… ghoulish I call it – they may as well ring up and say 'Oh! You're not dead yet? Got any plans?'"

"*No!*" I interrupted, "the message on my ansaphone was *not* from any of them. Not about computers, nor life insurance, I took a deep breath, "It was from my *lover!*"

"Oh!"

The remnant of the biscuit fell apart – most of it suddenly lay floating in her cup with just a scrap left held between fingers and thumb.

There was a bit of a pause.

We both looked at the section of biscuit floating in its mid-brown pool. As we watched, it up-ended and sank.

Angela said, "There are some custard creams! Would you like one?"

I said, "I *had* told him never to *do* that."

"Told who? To never what?" Angela went after

the drowned biscuit with a spoon but then thought better of it and abandoned the rescue.

"You mean 'whom' not 'who'," I corrected her, "Simon. I had told *Simon*." It was funny to be saying that name out loud to someone who was *not* Simon.

"Simon?"

"Simon."

"Simon is your… er… your…?"

"Lover, yes."

"Oh. You've never mentioned…?"

"No – I never did. Not the sort of thing one bandies about is it?"

"No."

"I didn't want to tell you – with you going through a divorce…"

"I'm not going through a divorce."

"Going through… whatever you call this then… I didn't want to tell you while you are going through this-brief – separation – while Martin – experiments – some more – with the man he's been – seeing – for three years (I'm not sure the experiments to develop vaccines took *that* long, by the way) – but I didn't want to tell you about. Well… Simon… Thought it might upset you."

"Right. Well. Like a refill?"

"Has it done?"

"Has what done... what?"

"Has my having an affair upset you?"

"Well... um... not sure... Yes, I think it *has*. Actually. Need time to think. Oh gosh. Gosh yes!" She stood up, "My world's suddenly gone all *shoogly*... Beth! Simon? *Beth*! What do you *mean* 'Lover'? *Why* have you got a lover? You can't just come in here and tell me you have a lover! What do you *mean*?" She sat down again.

The coffee jar in her hand was keeping time with her exclamations.

"Careful-you'll spill it."

"I don't *care* if I spill it! Oh drat! That'll stain! How? *How* have you got a lover? What do you mean *'lover'*? Pass me that cloth! How long's this been going on?"

"That's a song isn't it?"

"Yes. Marvin Gaye I think... Not one of his best though... I really like..."

"Four years," I muttered.

"Four *years*? *Four* years? *Four years*? You've been having an affair for *four years*?"

"Yes, four years," I agreed," It does sound a long time when you say it like that – nice round number though. Couldn't believe it either when I totted it up. Only meant to be a fling. A one- night stand. Sort of got into a habit."

"A *habit?*" She was staring at me as if I'd spat at her – although I hadn't.

"Yes, that's what I'd call it. A bad habit. A nice bad habit," I said.

"You couldn't just bite your nails or dunk biscuits in your coffee or chew your hair – like the rest of us? It had to be an extra marital affair did it? For four years?"

"Yes. Some bad habits take longer to develop than others. You have to work at them"

"And Frank's only just now found out?" She was aghast.

"Well, he's had a lot on his mind. Golf mostly."

"He *does* play a lot of golf," she observed.

"But not as much as I thought he did as it happens," I added.

"So… who's this 'Simon'?" She had finished wiping the coffee table and faced me with a raised cloth with coffee stains.

"Well, we just met and… it… went on from there."

"Did it? Did it *really?* I meet a *lot* of people, Beth, and it doesn't 'go on from there'. You're a married woman Beth!" She brandished the stained serviette at me to drive home the point.

"Believe me I *know*," I confided.

"Did you meet on a train?"

"No we didn't meet on a train. Why…?"

"Did…?"

"And, no, I didn't get soot in my eye and no, he isn't a doctor!"

"Ah."

"It was Pottery 101."

"Eh? I mean, what?"

"Pottery 101. My evening class. One of them. The first," I explained.

"Pottery? Oh like in *'Ghost'* on the pottery wheel – I've seen that – when they…"

"Angela this isn't a sodding *film*. This is real life!"

"Oh! Sorry. I just thought… Didn't you do that then – with all the clay going everywhere … and the hands?" she enquired, interestedly.

"We might have done that, yes, but that's not the point right now."

"You might have *told* me. I wondered why you were getting so good at pottery – making all those pots you kept giving me."

"I had to put them *somewhere*," I said, "and I didn't want Frank getting suspicious. It's why I never moved up from 101: Pottery for Beginners. I could make a pretty convincing Venus de Milo out of a handful of mud after three years. But all the advanced classes were in the morning – and that was no good to us – me and Simon."

"Simon and me," Angela corrected, "Yes, I noticed that you didn't make so much progress with cookery, or woodwork or Mandarin."

"No, well, lacked the motivation there. And missed quite a few classes – to be with Simon – the other classes were just alibis. He was a very good teacher."

"Oh?"

"Pottery – he's a *pottery* teacher, Angela. Part-time. He's amazing. I'm pretty good myself now actually."

"But you couldn't move into the advanced pottery classes?"

"Well no… they're all in the mornings – that would have been awkward – trying to meet up afterwards – lunchtimes – sordid you see – *and* daylight – so I stayed at Beginners 101 every term so we could be together in the evenings. I'd just pretend to be a beginner again at the start of every year with the new class. The other beginner students all thought I was a pottery *genius*. That was nice too."

"Why didn't you tell me?"

"How could I tell you? You've always believed in 'marriage vows forever' and all that... stuff ... and, well, so do I really, and you always said you *hated* women who 'went off the rails' you called it – you ended your friendship with Wendy when they split up – and then the golf club crowd might have found out or you might have told Martin and he might have told Frank... so I didn't tell *you*... Oh I don't know – I believe in those things too. Or I used to. It never felt the right time to tell you... would have made it all too *real* somehow – I just expected it to stop one day."

"You *expected* it to stop? Without you actually *stopping* it? You were expecting him to finish it then?"

"Oh god no – he's nuts about me. But I'd have had to make a decision."

"*And* you'd have had to give up pottery."

"Can we just forget the pottery?" I requested.

"Okay I'll try. And what about all your other evening classes – did you...?"

"No! I didn't cop off with someone from every class if that's what you're thinking. Nothing serious anyway. OK, I might have had the odd *fling* elsewhere, everyone does at evening classes – that's what they're for – nothing serious though – but with Simon it was different. It *is* different."

"Serious Simon?"

"Are you listening? But now he's blown it One *stupid* message. Do you think he did it in on purpose? He was always wanting me to tell Frank: 'Tell him, Beth – then we can be together. I'm sick of being the other man and living a lie', he'd say. Don't know what he thinks the rest of us are living."

"But how did you *do* this – where did you used to… er… meet – Is Simon married too?"

"Hell no! Lives with his parents."

"Oh! And how do you get on with them?"

"We never went *there*! Of course we never went there! We'd meet after class and go to nice little Bed and Breakfasts or a nice little tucked away hotel."

"That must have cost…"

"A fortune, yes! Didn't know affairs could be so expensive. Just as well I gave myself a pay rise."

"So he… this Simon… wants to be with you?"

"Of *course* he wants to be with me. He loves me. But he's had that!"

"You still love Frank?"

"Yes of course I do! Well no, actually. I just like what comes *with* Frank. There are certain advantages to being a solicitor's wife which my own income just wouldn't cover."

"Like being able to pay for dozens of evening classes?"

"Yes – and the little niceties in life."

"Like affairs in comfy little B&B's and tucked away hotels?" she suggested.

"Well yes – wouldn't want some sordid little bunk up in the car now would I?"

"Well, no," she agreed, "There *are* standards. And what does Simon do? When he's not potting? Or is it pottering?"

"He writes poetry, paints pictures. He's painted me you know. And in between he's... he's a..." I struggled to say it out loud, "an agency worker. You've probably seen him about the place planting things or digging things up or moving things or cleaning things... or... something."

"I see a lot of them about. In the...?" she mimed.

"Bright fluorescent jackets *yes*. *And* the big boots. Yes."

"Does he wear them when...?"

"When I ask him to yes."

"Hm. Sounds good!"

"It *was* good. Look, can we focus here – what am I going to *do*?" I didn't feel comfortable to be the one asking for support and advice.

"What's *Frank* going to do?" said Angela, "He's stormed off has he? Well... just don't tell him the *worst* of it –just tell him the minimum – don't mention the figure four – or *anything* about 'years' – say it was just a one off, a one-night fling, or a wild moment of passion after too much sherry – or that nothing *has* happened yet it was just somebody ringing up trying his luck…"

"That would be lying," I said.

"Well, yes… presumably you've been doing quite a lot of that?"

"But I've never actually *lied* to Frank."

"Hm? In four years?"

"I wish you'd stop saying four years. It makes it sound longer when you say it. No. I've never actually *said* 'I'm not having an affair' or 'I'm not seeing somebody else' or…."

"I'm not really going to my evening class tonight?"

"I went to *some* of them – you lose your place on the course otherwise that's how it worked – evening class and meet up afterwards. I didn't tell any lies!"

"How about 'Hey Frank – I'll be staying round at Angie's tonight to keep her company'?"

"Yes, well there might have been a few of those. But I *would* have stayed if you'd needed company so it wasn't a *real* lie."

"I feel used."

"Well! I had to try to keep you separate in case something slipped out – he'd think I was here when…"

"Actually you were in a three-star love nest. Well, better than the back of a car anyway – or in a wood."

"There aren't any woods around here – we looked. I did think of asking if we could come here but it didn't seem right somehow with you… going through…"

"A brief separation while Martin experiments with Allan, yes," she finished for me but without her previous conviction or enthusiasm.

"Wouldn't have seemed right to ask," I said.

"No, well I'd have felt really left out wouldn't I – you are *experimenting* with Simon, Martin with Allan – everybody *experimenting* around me like mad and having a fine old time – while I'm trying to do the right thing – and being dashed miserable!"

She put the coffee pot down quite forcefully. I had never heard her swear before.

"Well you *could* do experimenting too – I *did* try to get you interested," I said in my defence.

"Yes you did… I thought you were trying to help me get over Martin not just dragging me down to your level of depravity," she said, snootily, standing up again.

"Well you've missed your chance now," I said, standing too.

"Yes, and I *was* just coming around to the idea. Has Simon got a friend?"

"Look can we just focus on the fact my marriage has just hit the rocks?"

"Experimental rocks – like mine?"

"It's worse than that."

"So... Frank was a bit upset and stormed off? He heard Simon's message on the answerphone and hit the roof? Well you can see why – he's probably deeply hurt and feels betrayed and rejected and unloved and..."

"No – that's the bit I haven't told you about: he was *delighted*."

"What?" Angela looked bewildered.

"Oh it's the best bit! I haven't told you! Frank heard the message – Simon leaving a message about meeting me later at such and such hotel – *bit* of a giveaway – I can't believe Simon *didn't* do it on purpose – and – it's given Frank the excuse he needed."

"Excuse to do what?" she asked.

"To leave me."

"What? Oh he'll be back- he's just upset – you can

make it right – just tell him …" She was confident.

"No he won't – he left me years ago really. All that golf."

"That's just his hobby."

"But it *wasn't* just the golf – you see, he was… he was… carrying on all this time – behind my back with… with… the top golfer at the club!"

"Marion!?"

"Yes! Marion! Her with the cups and the medals and the six-below par average and the big arse! Marion!"

"Carrying on? Well did you never suspect anything?"

"Well why *would* I? I was always out with Simon or doing woodwork or whatever. I didn't have *time* to suspect anything! Two-timing bastard!"

"'Woodwork or whatever' Is that a new name for it? I can never keep up?" she asked.

"No! Don't be revolting! I *did* do 101 Woodwork actually – I made a birdbox- it's quite good too – but, yes, when I was at my evening classes he was at… well… it. With Marion. At her flat in town. They were never even at our house apparently!"

"Then you and Simon needn't have gone to a…?"

"Bed and breakfast – yes, I've thought of that. Could've saved a fortune!"

"Yes – pity that," she sympathised. "Or you could have all chipped in to share…or had a rota and taken it in turns."

"Don't be squalid. These are proper affairs not quickies!"

"I don't think I could do an affair," she was thoughtful, "Complicated. At least quickies are…"

"I don't want to talk about quickies!" I snapped.

"Oh, ok. So… um… you never knew?"

"No. All the time I was with Simon, Frank was off with Marion – being unfaithful to me – the lying, deceitful toad!"

"Don't toads mate for life?"

"I don't know! Probably. Or they pretend to and the next minute they're round the back of the bulrushes with the floozie of the pond."

"Don't think anyone says 'floozie' any more. More tea?"

"What am I going to *do*?"

"Well you could put the biccie on a plate and I'll give you a tray."

"No, I meant…"

"And let's sit down again – may as well be comfy."

"Ok. Mm, this is nice. Is it decaf? What shall I do about my marriage?"

"What do you *want* to do?" she said, practically.

"Go back to before that message."

"Hmm, tricky. Biccie?"

"Everything was going so *well* then," I moaned.

"Sounds like it!"

"Work was going okay – Interesting evening classes – some of them…"

"Some more interesting than others…?" she muttered darkly.

"… Seeing Simon… Frank happy with his golf and his work."

"Just a bit happier than you thought he was. Sorry. Is *she* married as well?"

"Who?"

"Marion."

"I don't know. Why?"

"Just a loose end that's all. I like a plot where all the loose ends are…"

"Angie, this isn't a plot – this is a life – *my* life."

"Of course – yes. Bound to be a bit messy."

"Not messy – *interesting*. My life is *interesting*."

"Yes of course it is, Beth. I'm all agog. See?"

"I have to be positive. I'm too old to wallow in

self-pity."

"No one's ever *that* old."

"I wish I knew what to do. When I was young I always knew what to *do*."

"No one's ever that *young*. Are you sure your memory isn't editing things a bit – looking back?" asked Angie.

"Maybe, yes. Maybe I've really spent my whole life blundering about wondering what the hell is going on? I just put on a good front."

"Sums it up for me. Refill?"

"Yeh, go on."

"It'll work out, you see," said Angela, comfortably, "Have you asked Simon – why he *left* that message? *He's* caused all the trouble."

"Haven't seen him yet. It's quite put me off him really. He always *said* he wanted to bring things to a head – 'force my hand'. I never thought he'd actually *do* it though. I've always *said* I'd tell Frank, leave him, move in with Simon and all that but I never *meant* it of course! Why would I want to leave Frank? It's such a beautiful house!"

"I've always thought so," she agreed.

"Big garden – patio – great for parties!"

"You never had any parties," she pointed out.

"Yes I know *that* – but I always felt we *could* have parties – if we wanted to I mean. We just never got around to it."

"Well I can see why you didn't! How would you have had time in between…"

"Will you stop going on about it?" I protested.

"Going *on* about it? I've just found out you've been lying to me all this time…!" she protested.

"I never lied!"

"Well, been highly economical with the truth then if you like – and there's this whole other life I didn't know anything about going on right under my nose…!" she complained.

"It wasn't a whole life – just an affair with someone I like being with. On the *edges* of life. Anyway –*you* never had parties either."

"Of course not – not proper parties anyway. Martin didn't like parties – said they intruded on his 'personal space'."

"Did they?" I asked.

"God yes! He needed more personal space than a beached whale. We had dinner parties though. You and Frank and the golfers at some – then others with all his psychology cronies from college and HR and *their* partners – and they were all psychologists or psychiatrists too. We'd eat and then they'd all sit around analysing me. I was the only one there who wasn't a shrink."

"Oh dear!"

"I didn't enjoy it much," she confessed.

"You party pooper you! Most of us have to pay good money to have somebody rake us over and tell us why we're getting it wrong.

And at least you *had* parties even if you didn't enjoy them."

"Dinner parties aren't real parties – just people sitting around – troughing."

"Well that's one way of looking at it."

"They'd decide on all my neuroses. And then we'd have pudding. I don't think I'm any good in social situations."

"I don't think anybody is really."

"I just get all nervous when I'm socialising and talk rubbish."

"Isn't that what we all do? That's what socialising *is* isn't it?"

"But why do we *do* it?"

"Well we have to do *something*. Only natural."

"Herpes is natural."

"Don't be vulgar! And are you sure you want to

get back to that life with Martin – it doesn't sound all that great actually."

"It passed the time."

"Well, time *does* pass. But what if Martin stays with Allan – maybe this is *it* for him. They have been seeing each other for three years after all."

"Well –you've been seeing Simon for four! You said yourself – maybe it's just a habit that got out of hand – it'll end any day now and we can get back to normal. You don't want to be with Simon even after... so many years – so I bet Martin will get fed up with Allan after three and come back here!"

"I don't think you can rely on that. You told me – they *have* been seen together in the canteen – sharing pudding!"

"It's a sign of their relationship coming to an end. Anyway, this isn't about me, this is about you. What are *you* going to do?"

"I don't know. I don't know if Frank will want to leave me for Marion really."

"That would leave you free to move in with Simon. Or he could move in with you?"

"I don't think Simon and me know each other well enough for a big move like that."

"Simon and *I*," she corrected, "You don't know each other? After four... all that time?" That four number again you didn't want me to mention. That 'years' thing. Lots of time to get to know each other!"

"It's not *that* much!" I insisted.

"I think it's *quite* much. I think it's in the region of 'much'," she insisted.

"No. Not really. Not when you look at it."

"Look at it? From what angle?" she challenged.

"Well it's not *really* four years – you see – just the *evenings* of four years. Twice a week. And some nights."

"And the occasional 'morning after' I bet. Mornings after are where you *really* get to know somebody I reckon."

"Not if you get to the door quick enough in the early hours – and get showered and changed at work."

"Did you…?"

"Oh yes. I'm not one for the grey reality of dawn myself. Kept a change of clothes at work and just went in early. Gave myself a bonus for being keen!"

"Okay, four years of evenings – how often?"

"Two or three times a week. Except when one of us was away on holiday."

"You with Frank?"

"Yes – we go on river cruises a few times a year."

"And Simon?"

"He'd go with his mum and dad to Bognor so we'd miss a week – but we'd always make up for it when we got back – so it sort of evens out."

"Twice a week, evenings and nights together. So what does that add up to? I'll get my calculator."

"I mean – it's not the *quantity* of time – you can't measure it – but we just shared the *passion* – the *special* times. Not the rest of it."

"The rest of it?"

"Yes – Simon and me… I… did all the sexy stuff, the new positions and the sex toys, the passion and the heat, the outfits – all the sweat and soapy showers and the…"

"Clay?"

"Can we forget the clay?"

"I am trying to."

"We just did the special times but we didn't…"

"Didn't what?"

"We never went to the garden centre. We never bickered over the shopping list or whose turn it was to put the trash out or whose snoring was the worst. Simon and I have rarely slept a whole night together.

Couldn't really, he'd be on 'earlies' – cleaning or weeding somewhere or guarding something."

"Doesn't sound like you slept at all – all those soapy showers!"

"You know what I mean! Intimacy is not just about… *that*. Frank and I had something special."

"Yeh, a nice big house with a patio. Simon was just your bit on the side in his wellies!" she summarised.

"He does look good in his wellies – Well, yeh – I like – liked- – him – a lot – but just *fancied* him really. We couldn't build a *life* together."

"Why? Doesn't he play golf?"

"No. He wouldn't fit in down the golf club. Mows it sometimes. Seen him. Had to pretend we didn't know each other."

"Well that's *that* then! If he wouldn't fit in down the golf club…"

"It was time for it to end. We can both move on."

"Is Simon married too?"

"Oh god no! He's only 26."

"26!"

"Yes what's wrong with 26? I was 26 once. And you were too."

"Yes, but we haven't been for quite a while."

"Age makes no difference," I declared.

"How could you be happy with a 26-year-old?"

"Do you want me to write you a list?"

"No – that's not... But isn't he going to be very upset if you just finish with him? After four years?"

"Oh he'll bounce back – find someone his own age. I think he just liked my glamorous sophistication, my worldly wisdom, my elegant lifestyle…"

"… And having it off in hotels. At his age he should still be doing it in the backs of cars. You've ruined him!"

"No some bright young thing will help him lick his…"

"Careful!"

"Wounds! You'll see. He'll be looking for a new love – he'll find one. Youth will have its way I'll be just discarded, thrown away like a used sock!"

"I think you need to keep in mind who's doing the discarding here. He left that message wanting to be with you," she pointed out, unhelpfully.

"Oh he *thinks* he's in love with me but he's too young to know what love is."

"And too poor to get a decent mortgage. That's that then."

"Enough about me. What's new with you anyway?" I said.

"Well, bit difficult to follow *that* really. Let's see, I

got a new box set of 'Ealing Comedies' and tried a new chicken dish from Raja's but other than that…."

"No news about Martin and Allan?"

"Well… yes… Saw them in the canteen again last Thursday. Didn't see them sharing pudding. It was a mixed salad. They got up and left when they saw me. Cowards! Eating salad together in public…"

"How did you feel?"

"Okay actually. Maybe I am moving on like you said?"

"You're finding your feet?

"Well, maybe there *are* other fish in the sea after all. My lodger never seems to go without and she seems quite happy being single."

"Tenant."

"Yeh, whatever. So – what now?"

"Dunno. Frank'll have to move out – find a flat or move in with Marion," I speculated.

"Simon finding a new love, me finding my feet, Frank finding a new flat – bit like the *Wizard of Oz* isn't it?"

"Yes – wish we *could* just turn up somewhere and ask for what we need from some big, phoney, magic person. But I never was religious."

"Another coffee?"

"Yeh go on. I suppose it'll be the same for Frank after a while."

"Hm?"

"With Marion. From glamour and exciting secrets to everyday humdrum, suddenly. Mind you, it's not the first time he's strayed," I confessed.

"Really? You never said."

"Well – people don't talk about that sort of stuff do we? If we did, nobody would invite you to their dinner parties. Yes – we went through a bad patch. He hit his forties and decided he didn't want to."

"Didn't want to what?"

"Hit his 40s."

"You never said."

"Well, you and Martin and everybody else I knew seemed so happy and I felt such an idiot so I didn't tell anyone. He took off with a twenty-something trainee in his firm."

"Ah! Probably swept her off her feet with his experience and maturity. He can look quite sophisticated in a suit."

"Didn't last."

"What happened?"

"Well, I confronted her and she told me I was stifling him – that he 'wanted to travel the world and find his soul and the *real* meaning of life' and that she was going to go with him: They'd 'be free together and explore everything the world has to offer' and 'be the free spirits who are brave enough to face its challenges'. I was quite impressed," I remembered.

"So did they? Head off into the sunset and go and explore the world?"

"Briefly," I said, "They didn't get far. Frank had talked to her of 'exploring the world' and 'seeking out adventures' and 'to hell with the well-beaten track and convention' and seeing all the great sights in every continent – but he had failed to mention *one* little word. He told her he was going to seek out his soul – but he didn't tell her where he was going to *look* – one little word – and that word put paid to the whole plan. Her love for him turned up its heels and died on the spot."

"What word?"

"The word 'tent'. He hadn't sort of mentioned it. He wanted to get back to his youth – scout camps and living rough – but she had been thinking more along the lines of five-star resorts – the two didn't *quite* fit."

"Poor Frank!"

"Poor Frank nothing. She vanished in a cloud of dust and he came home with his tail between his legs. We took off for a camping tour of Canada and that got it out of his system no problem. He was happy as Larry – until we woke up one morning to find a great grizzly chewing its way through our supply tent. We de-camped at the double to the nearest city and a decent hotel – the wild seemed to lose its appeal for him after that. Thank god!"

"I remember you telling me about the grizzly – but you never said about the twenty-something."

"Some stories are better told than others. We scuttled back to Montreal and lived it up in comfort until our flight back home. Been fine ever since – 'til now."

"Well, until four-years ago and 'Simon 101'".

"That was no threat to our marriage! It was just a fling that got a bit out of hand. Did you ever go camping?" I asked, needing a change of subject.

She frowned. "Only once when we were kids. Mum and Dad took us all up the mountains. One of Dad's 'get back to Nature, closer to God' phases."

"Good?"

"Not really. We all got bitten by midges by day and fleas by night."

"Right. That would put you off."

"Yes. Dad took it as a sign. He was convinced that if you joined up all the bites on my face it would spell 'Jesus'. He was going through one of his religious phases," she reminisced.

"Oh right. And did it?"

"Mum wouldn't let him. Then my brother got hold of the felt pen first to join them up and spelt out something quite rude."

"Oh dear!"

"Took a week to scrub off. They never bothered with camping after that and my dad gave up religion too. *And* I got a week off school so it wasn't all bad. So... Frank should be back soon. Like Martin. He won't want this 'new life' in a flat?" she queried.

"Especially not with someone who plays better golf than he does," I mused.

"Can't see it going down well at his firm either – leaving his wife," she guessed.

"They wouldn't be bothered, "I shook my head," And Frank *hates* being a solicitor anyway so even if he was struck off he'd just see it as a chance to escape."

"What? Again? Has he forgotten about the grizzly then?"

"Not camping. But to a different job. He was always moaning about his work."

"But it's really well paid – most people would *love* to be a solicitor!"

"Not him. 'Oh why is my life so meaningless and

empty? Why did I end up in this hellhole of a job? What's it all for I ask you?'" I gave an impression of Frank in a mope.

"That does sound a bit negative," Angela agreed.

"Oh no, that's just for openers! Then he'd go into the warm up: 'I *could* have been *some*body! Somebody that mattered, somebody that *did* things, somebody who doesn't spend his days wading through bits of paper and other people's lives. '… wasted! My life is wasted! I never had a *chance*! Push, push, push the next exam the next step on the greasy ladder was I meeting the right people? Was I eating at the right restaurants? The highest salary – the most expensive car – a house like a mausoleum – what's it all *for*? Where did my youth *go*? Smoking marijuana and wild parties and talking about interesting ideas and having affairs? Never did anything for me! But did anyone try to *help*? It's too late now – got a mortgage now, and two cars. And a Summer house. Holidays to pay for, *and* a boat! Oh god when I think what might have been…', I knew it by heart having heard it so often, and by then he's usually slumped in a chair, outside of three large whiskies," I concluded.

"I didn't know you had a Summer house – why didn't you and Simon…?"

"Damp. And the roof needs fixing."

"Ah! Frank wasn't happy then? What *did* he want

out of life? What '*might* have been?' I always thought you two were reasonably happy?"

"We were – just separately reasonably happy."

"You had rows? I never saw."

"Well of course you wouldn't *see*! That's what doors are for! Of course we did – yes! Sometimes I'd want to slap him. But he's a solicitor. He'd say 'you're just conforming to statistics Bethany, – 90% of all violence happens inside the home'. Pompous arse! So I'd say 'fine, let's go in the garden and I'll hit you there –start a new trend'."

"Right. So his job got him down then? It seems so glamorous, so… je ne sais quoi."

"Nobody says 'je ne sais quoi' anymore."

"Why not?"

"I don't know."

"Well, so… successful then."

"Success? How do you measure that? It's only a *success* if it's where you *want* to be. And he didn't"

"Where did he want to be then?"

"I was just coming to that bit – he always ended with that… he'd say 'I could have been in a *real* job' he'd say – 'out at dawn in the new day – back in the dusk after a good day down the pit –feeling pleasantly tired. I was deprived'!"

"I'm not sure people *are* pleasantly tired after eight hours down the pit," Angela said.

"I *know*! I would point that out but he wouldn't hear me, 'real work, with real people, with sweat on their brow not eight million tons of paperwork and hours on the golf course with the boss. Or in a factory – I could have been stuffing chickens –making food – the basic needs of human life, real work…!'. I'd say – Frank, £7 an hour wouldn't meet the 'basic needs' of *your* life it wouldn't even cover your golfing fees, 'but he never listened, on he'd go,' *real* people, *real* work, making things, delivering things, stuffing things…"

"With sweat on their brows?" she interjected.

"Definitely, that was a recurring theme. *Real* sweat on *real* brows mind you. I told him, the only time he had sweat on his brow was when we were in the sauna. He hated doing physical work really – only got all romantic about it when it was other people doing it. He was a great believer in sweaty brows so long as his own was *not* among them. He wouldn't listen, just said I didn't understand him. Then he'd hit the Glenfiddich and go all quiet until bedtime."

"Do you think he *will* find his true self?"

"Hope not for his sake – it's bad enough when he finds a spider in the bath."

"And so… you took to evening classes?"

"Well, home life *did* get a bit repetitive. I mean nobody likes their job do they – I don't like selling houses to people. I don't like the houses and I don't like the people I sell them to – but we do it for the money don't we? I mean what's it matter who owns a house or doesn't own it?

Doesn't change the world does it? People sell a house, buy another one – I mean there's no *point* in that but you don't hear me bellyaching about it Someone's got to do it or houses wouldn't get sold and they'd be no use to anybody then would they?"

"No, of course not. But if Frank would like a job using his hands and all that – with sweat on his brow…"

"Yes?"

"Well maybe you could introduce him to Simon and he could find him something at the agency – doing the verges or whatever?" she suggested.

"Angela, that isn't going to *happen*. Frank is *not* going to dig ditches or plant flowers or do anything *useful* with his life – we can't afford the drop in income – nor is he going to move in with Miss Golfing Floozy – it's just another fling! He'll finish with her and I'll finish with Simon and we'll all be back as we were – we'll go on a river cruise and forget all about it."

"Good plan!"

"Well what about Martin," I asked, "– you're alright with your job but does Martin like *his* job? Psychiatrist or psychologist or whatever he is? Counselling people?"

"Hell no! Especially when he'd had a few. He sometimes likes analysing people – especially me if we'd had a row – but when he'd had a few glasses of wine it would all come out then."

"Ooh! What would?" I was all ears again.

"His dream. His secret dream."

"Oh yeh? Do tell. Some far-out raunchy fantasy I expect?"

"Not really. Bus driver. He wanted to be a bus driver."

"Oh. Bus driver?" I felt quite disappointed, again.

"He'd get quite explicit."

"Oh?"

"Yes… 'Ding ding, plenty of room at the back." Double decker it had to be too – and lots of sixpenny returns."

"Six-penny returns? Quite an old bus then, in this dream?"

"Yes, and helping people with their shopping and driving all around town ringing the bell all seemed to be a big part of it too. I got quite used to it. Just nodded and looked as if I was listening until he fell asleep. He'd end up saying he was in agony, 'spiritual agony'. I'd tell him not to be so silly, bus drivers don't earn enough — *and* point out he's in quite a *well-padded* agony, relatively speaking. Then he would get more cross and say was 'a well-padded agony' the best we can hope for? Which is a bit silly again — because I suppose it *is*."

"I suppose we all have our dreams, "I commiserated.

"And then we'd have a row and he'd end up saying it was all because I'm 'psychologically inadequate'.""

"That doesn't sound very nice — psychoanalysing you all the time. Didn't that get you down?"

"Sometimes. Especially when he said I was sexually repressed."

"Oh? Did he?"

"Yes, when I wanted a cuddle. He didn't like cuddles. Made him 'uncomfortable.'""

"Really?"

"Yes, he'd say 'for Christ's sake Angie, I'm a *psychiatrist*, I'm a Freudian — I've studied the human mind and the female body — I've spent years reading *everything* there is to know about the act of human copulation, the body's higher planes of ecstasy, the frontiers of pleasure and how to cross them — I know every position there is and you come here and want a *cuddle*! Just what kind of pervert am I married to?'

He seemed to think sex was like starting a car: press button A, switch lever on, start ignition... go through the gears – orgasm!"

"Gosh did you?"

"Oh yes, had to, I've seen what he's like when the car won't start."

"You weren't 'repressed' then?"

"No, just bored now I come to think of it. People aren't just bodies are they? Maybe I should have had a Simon. Maybe all this 'together forever' stuff isn't all it's cracked up to be. Well Martin's took off – with his Allan – maybe I should too?"

"You've changed your tune?"

"Well... I've been thinking."

"Careful, that can be dangerous!"

"Well..." she hesitated, "it was when I saw them in the canteen on Thursday – what they were doing, just before they started on the salad – it made me realise..."

"Why? What on Earth were they doing?" I was interested, but by now I'd learned not to get excited.

"They were having a cuddle."

"Oh! It's just a *fling* though – you said. Him and Allan."

"No," she said, "it's not a fling. I saw that then. He looked... well... not laughing or falling about... Just, well... happy. Maybe our marriage *has* come to the end of its story. Not Martin's fault – he's just fallen in love with someone else. Happens to be Allan. He always thought being gay was wrong because Freud said so but maybe it *is* just... love? I 'm going to have to rethink a few other things I believed in too because they don't make much sense either when you look at them properly..."

"You said it was just a fling?"

"Hmm! –three years though – and they've moved in together. You were having 'a fling' for even longer with Simon – and you can leave *him* – it isn't the length of time is it – it's how you feel about someone. Our marriage was quite boring really now I come to look at it. It was just a habit."

"A habit that took its time?"

She pulled a face. "So maybe our spouses running off with other people is a *good* thing? Maybe we'll look back and see that this was actually the best thing that could have happened. Now we have to start again."

"But aren't we too old to start again?"

"No one ever gets *that* old. You just have to keep going, keep living, until closing time. *Then* you're too old."

"What's all that stuff?"

"Oh that's the lodger's – she's clearing out all her old videos and DVDs – got into 'streaming – *and* she's moving to a new place."

"Oh, I didn't know."

"Neither did I until last night. I used to feel sorry for her, thought she was living wrong.. Now I'm not so sure. Suited her. And I *am* going to retrain... or something – my job is just about making people miserable – I've had enough of that – that's rubbish too, now I look at it. I want a job where I can be helpful and nice!"

"Angela – those sorts of jobs don't *pay!*" I said, horrified.

"Well, I'll need to do *something-* this is going to be a new me! This job pays but really it's the worst job I've ever had."

"What was the *best* job you ever had then?"

She thought for a minute. "It wasn't a job – I was a volunteer. Part of my training – only a week's placement – Business Studies – the Third Sector – helping out with a singing group up at the hospital. People with dementia. Singing. They couldn't talk anymore but they would sing. They would hear an old song from their youth – and they would suddenly start singing! I put the CDs on and led – using a song sheet. Amazing. It made me feel… Oh… what 's the word…?"

I had a guess, "Embarrassed?"

"No," she said.

"Scared? Nauseated?" I guessed again.

"No… Needed, it made me feel needed. For a whole week," she said, "I'd like to feel that again."

"But your parents haven't *got* dementia — they don't need a singing group?"

"No, but somebody else's mother might," she said.

"My turn to put the kettle on," I said, "Is the new you going to quit watching films then?" I felt rather unnerved.

"No — I won't be *that* new. I'll keep the bits I like. This came in the post."

It was a large brown envelope.

"It's a course in Film Studies, online," she said, "I've enrolled. A job pays the bills but I may as well do stuff I like outside of it — singing old songs and studying films – could be good "

I had to admit I was impressed if a little alarmed.

Then I stepped into the kitchen and had to take a step back in surprise and horror.

"You've done something to your kitchen, Angela! Is that a new sideboard? All covered in dishes?"

"That? No, Beth, that's the sink."

"I think your dishes need doing!"

"No they don't. They're quite happy until I need them again. Plenty more in the cupboard." She was quite matter of fact.

"Is that a gravy boat?" I pointed.

"Yes, it stands in nicely as a cereal bowl. I've used all the others."

"Angela – are your standards slipping?"

"No, they were never *my* standards. Always somebody else's. It's nice not having to make everything look nice all the time."

As we stood there the doorbell rang and Angela went to answer it. I heard voices and she returned with a large box which she opened and put on the table.

"And what's that? It looks like a piece of tapestry?" I pointed – my hand wasn't exactly trembling but it wasn't far off.

"It's a pizza. That'll be tea," she said.

"Oh!"

"Vegetarian – low salt and all that – very healthy!"

"Angela!"

"I've realised – I *hate* cooking. Always did. And I can afford deliveries. Easy system – pay check comes in – Martin's money for the mortgage comes in – I phone out for pizzas. *And* curries. You should try it. Mind you, no rent coming in will make a difference now."

"I think I need to sit down. What's *happened* to you?" I asked.

"Don't know. I'm getting de-Martin'd I think. He *hated* pizza. I think maybe I've always been like this: inside the house-proud workaholic was a completely happy slob – fighting to get out. Well, now she's out!

I tried being the perfect little housewife – look where that got me – well they can stuff it!"

"Well…!"

"Don't worry, I *will* do the dishes eventually, when I *want* to. When *I* want to. I feel a whole new life evolving – like a phoenix in the ashes."

"Sure it isn't a whole new *ecosystem* evolving – in your sink? There *is* such a thing as typhoid you know."

"Hygiene is overrated – our immune system needs germs to keep it strong. Like to stay for some pizza?"

"Er, no thanks. You *do* seem more relaxed. You're not wearing any makeup!"

"No, I'm letting my skin breathe. I *am* more relaxed: keeping a crummy marriage together, keeping a job together, keeping the kitchen clean, cooking healthy meals, trying to look twenty years younger, keeping up with my family, psychoanalysing myself – and for what? No wonder I was tired all the time! No energy for doing anything *I* wanted to do. Now I've got the energy to do other things – now I'm back in my own life – I can go out, explore the world!"

"Oh great, where are we going?"

"Just because I *can*, doesn't mean I *want* to... I'm going to watch a film tonight – finish *'Groundhog Day'* and then pick another one from this pile," she gestured to a tottering pile on a shelf.

"You've seen all those films before though haven't you?" I queried.

"I've drunk wine before too. No reason not to do it again!"

She had a point.

I spotted *'Titanic'* in the pile and pointed it out. It had been a favourite of mine.

"Ooh no!" said Angela, "too *sad! He's* adventurous, caring and creative – and gorgeous – she's selfish and boring – and guess what happens? What does *that* tell you? I couldn't watch past that bit."

"But she *changes*," I said, spotting the flaw, "you should watch the rest of it. She becomes a different person!"

"Oh!" Angela looked surprised, "So... she stops being selfish and boring?"

"Well no, she carries on being selfish – but not quite so boring," I clarified.

"Oh," she looked disappointed. "Still," she brightened, "one out of two isn't bad!"

I had to agree.

She went on, thoughtfully, "Something like that *would* change you. If you let it."

"As long as you didn't drown," I agreed.

"And she must have got out from under all those horrible people too…" she added.

"*Were* they horrible people?" I queried. "I thought they were just very well dressed?" I felt uneasy.

But she didn't even waver.

"Fancy having a glass of wine and watching it?" she said, "I didn't *know* there was a happy ending!"

"Well, about 300 people die because a ship was trying to break a record and only had first class lifeboats – so it isn't *too* cheerful- but, yes, okay," I accepted the invitation. "But you don't fancy going *out* this evening? It *is* Saturday."

"No," she was being unnervingly decisive again, "I've been 'out' before – I know what's out there – it can *stay* there. I know you think I spend too much time watching films – but maybe I spend too much time trying to cope with life – not *enough* time watching films. Films are *great*. Even if one lets you

317

down you can just fast forward or switch it off and switch to another one! We've both tried our best at life – and look what it's done to us in return!"

"Well we haven't stopped yet have we?" I declared. "Have you thought maybe you're *afraid* of life? Of seeing the world?"

"Well of *course* I am – I'm bloody terrified! Life and the world – have you *seen* the state of them? There *is* something wrong with the whole set up. Why did I put up with Martin all these years except that I was scared – scared of being alone – scared of not being married? Why? Well *not* anymore!! There are worse things than being alone – like not being in your own *life*! I've got a lot of catching up to do! And it starts *now*!"

I was quite impressed – and taken aback. All sorts of unexpected futures seemed to suddenly open up as possibilities for this new and adventurous Angela doing courses and making decisions.

"What are you going to do?" I was almost afraid to ask.

Her eyes glittered with intent, "After this we're going to watch *'Malcolm X'*, *'Bend It Like Beckham'*, *'Chicken Run'* and *'Pride'*!" she announced.

"What the hell are *they*?" I wrinkled my nose, elegantly of course.

"Films I heard the shop steward going on about."

"Isn't she that *mad* woman at your place?" I queried.

"Well... maybe she isn't... I've been thinking... some of the things she says..."

"I've warned you against that. Thinking never did *me* any good," I said. I was quite alarmed.

"Well, they might be worth a look." she insisted, "My *whole* life has changed, I'll have to change my films too! And I'm going to be studying them now!"

"Well, I suppose that's one way... Maybe *I* could move in here – maybe I could be your new lodger? I don't want to be in that big house all alone. Hmm, maybe I *won't* finish with Simon after all. I *do* like being with him," I admitted, surprised to hear myself say that.

"You're blushing!" Angela pointed out, gleefully, "And why not? You like him – he likes you! Maybe we just have to accept there are some things we're *not* good at: You're not very good at golf – and I'm not very good at *life* – or at least not the one I've been leading – so now I'll lead another one -So... pass the remote and let's do something I *am* good at. Pizza?"

"Er actually, yes please, I'll give it a try."

I felt the world changing around me.

"Make yourself comfy – Red or white?"

"Er, red. Please!"

"Biccie? And a coffee as a chaser?"

"Marvellous!"

"Here goes!"

She pressed the remote.

The End

Printed in Great Britain
by Amazon